BAD HOMBRE

'Peace officer here!' Melnick barked, lunging from his place of concealment behind Alice. 'Stand right where you are!'

Although the deputy held his revolver and had delivered the mandatory words of command, he wondered if they had caught the right man. Standing just beyond the glow of the convertible's headlights, gold-rimmed spectacles glinting like the windows of a diver's helmet, the small, insignificant figure looked about as harmless as a new-born baby.

And responded with the devastating speed of a striking sidewinder!

Moving as swiftly as either deputy had ever seen it done, the man went into the F.B.I. combat crouch. Flashing from behind his back, his right hand aimed a Luger automatic pistol by instinctive alignment. Twice flame spurted from the muzzle. Caught in the chest and head by the two 9mm bullets, Melnick pitched over the back rest of the seat and on to the rear of the car.

Books by J. T. EDSON
Arranged in chronological order of stories

29. COMANCHE

Civil War Stories

30. THE FASTEST GUN IN TEXAS
58. KILL DUSTY FOG!
21. THE DEVIL GUN
63. UNDER THE STARS AND BARS
26. THE COLT AND THE SABRE
1. THE REBEL SPY
35. THE BLOODY BORDER
62. BACK TO THE BLOODY BORDER

The Floating Outfit Stories

4. THE YSABEL KID
56. .44 CALIBRE MAN
64. A HORSE CALLED MOGOLLON
50. GOODNIGHT'S DREAM
51. FROM HIDE AND HORN
THE HIDE AND TALLOW MEN†
21. THE HOODED RIDERS
12. QUIET TOWN
11. TRAIL BOSS
37. WAGONS TO BACKSIGHT
48. TROUBLED RANGE
52. SIDEWINDER
20. RANGELAND HERCULES
17. MCGRAW'S INHERITANCE
38. THE HALF-BREED
44. THE WILDCATS
2. THE BAD BUNCH
66. HELL IN THE PALO DURO
67. GO BACK TO HELL*
54. THE FAST GUN
43. CUCHILO
THE SOUTH WILL RISE AGAIN†
9. A TOWN CALLED YELLOWDOG
41. TRIGGER FAST
46. THE TROUBLE BUSTERS
25. THE MAKING OF A LAWMAN
28. THE LAW OF THE GUN
42. THE PEACEMAKERS
SET A-FOOT†
57. THE RUSHERS
47. THE FORTUNE HUNTERS
7. THE HARD RIDERS
14. THE RIO HONDO KID
16. WACO'S DEBT
3. THE TEXAN
34. THE FLOATING OUTFIT
55. APACHE RAMPAGE
8. RIO GUNS
60. RIO HONDO WAR
40. GUNSMOKE THUNDER
45. THE MAN FROM TEXAS
32. GUN WIZARD
36. THE SMALL TEXAN
31. THE TOWN TAMERS
53. RETURN TO BACKSIGHT
27. TERROR VALLEY
15. GUNS IN THE NIGHT

Waco Stories

24. SAGEBRUSH SLEUTH
5. ARIZONA RANGER
37. WACO RIDES IN
6. THE DRIFTER
DOC LEROY M.D.†
49. HOUND DOG MAN

Calamity Jane Stories

33. COLD DECK, HOT LEAD
18. CALAMITY SPELLS TROUBLE
19. TROUBLE TRAIL
22. THE BULL WHIP BREED
10. THE COW THIEVES
61. WHITE STALLION, RED MARE
13. THE BIG HUNT
THE WHIP AND THE WAR LANCE†

John Slaughter Stories

59. SLAUGHTER'S WAY
SLAUGHTER'S NEIGHBOURS†

Rockabye County Stories

THE PROFESSIONAL KILLERS
THE ¼ SECOND DRAW
THE DEPUTIES
POINT OF CONTACT
THE OWLHOOT
RUN FOR THE BORDER
BAD HOMBRE
THEY CALL IT PROGRESS†

Waxahachie Smith Stories

65. SLIP GUN
CURE THE TEXAS FEVER†

† In preparation. * Awaiting publication
and published by CORGI BOOKS

J T EDSON

BAD HOMBRE

CORGI BOOKS
TRANSWORLD PUBLISHERS LTD
A National General Company

BAD HOMBRE

A CORGI BOOK 0 552 08841 2

First publication in Great Britain

PRINTING HISTORY
Corgi edition published 1971

This book is set in 10 on 10½pt Intertype Baskerville

Corgi Books are published by Transworld
Publishers Ltd.,
Cavendish House, 57–59 Uxbridge Road,
Ealing, London, W.5.
Made and printed in Great Britain by
Cox & Wyman Ltd.,
London, Reading and Fakenham

For Sonja Pickers and the members of Melton Mowbray's Weight Watchers, who have helped me regain my sylph-like figure.

CHAPTER ONE

To a student of the Old West, as portrayed by Hollywood in the days when that town made movies for the entertainment and enjoyment of the public, the offices of the Rockabye County sheriff and his deputies in Gusher City would have been a disappointment. Located on the third floor of the modern, six-storey Department of Public Safety Building, the rooms looked nothing like the scene to which countless western movies had accustomed their audiences. Only the title of the department remained as visual evidence that the deputies' squadron, Watch Commander's and sheriff's offices were occupied by a traditional type of Texas peace officers. Apart from the name, the whole set-up might have been housing a New York, Chicago or Los Angeles detective squad, or it could even have been a field office of the Federal Bureau of Investigation.

Certainly the deputies' squadron had nothing of the traditional Old West about it. A large, well ventilated and illuminated room, it had eight modern desks, each with a typewriter and telephone extension, forming two lines across its centre. Several filing cabinets occupied much of the wall space, hinting at a more thorough organization than was usually shown by Old West lawmen. On one side of the double doors of the main entrance hung a bulletin board, with wanted posters, routine orders and other items of information pinned to it. At the other side of the doors, beneath the Duty Roster board – which allowed the Watch Commander to tell at a glance how many deputies he had at his disposal – the Office Log lay open and ready for use on a table. Flanking the door to the Watch Commander's office, two large boxes held the department's assault armament – Winchester Model 12 riot guns, Thompson submachine guns, telescope sighted sniper's rifles and Federal gas-shell dischargers – and a supply of ammunition for each type of weapon.

Times, methods and accommodation might change, but one aspect of Western law enforcement remained constant. On occasion, the jet-age peace officers needed firearms to carry out their duties.

That need was anything but apparent as First Deputy Ricardo Alvarez stepped out of the Watch Commander's office at five minutes past eleven on the warm summer's Monday night and looked around the squadron. Only two of his eight deputies were present; but, fortunately, they were the pair he had hoped to see. As he had listened to the telephone message which brought him into the squadroom, Alvarez had known which of his four teams he would send if they were available. Yet he still needed a moment to brace himself for what he had to do. Even though he knew Woman Deputy Joan Hilton was an efficient and capable peace officer with considerable practical experience, he still found difficulty in ordering her to go and face the unpleasant, often nauseating sights to be expected when investigating a homicide. However, personal considerations aside, he felt sure that the buxom blonde and her stocky, college educated, full-blood Comanche partner were the best team to handle the case of homicide which had just been brought to his attention.

'Joan, Sam,' Alvarez said. 'Are you free?'

'I wish we could say "no" to that,' Joan Hilton answered, glancing at the wall clock. In another fifty-five minutes, the Night Watch would be officially over. 'What's up, Ric?'

'Lasher have just turned in a "woman down" report,' the Night Watch Commander replied. 'Seventeen, Dick Street. Do you know it?'

'It's in Mockingbird Grove,' the blonde said quietly. 'I live out that way. Is there anything more on it?'

'Looks like she was beaten to death and robbed,' Alvarez answered, trying to keep his voice hard and impersonal. 'That's all we have so far.'

'Let's go, Sam,' Joan suggested. 'The sooner we get there, the quicker we'll know more. How about a photographer, Ric?'

'He'll be going with the S.I.B. crew,' Alvarez promised. 'The m.e. and ambulance have already been dispatched.'

'We may as well get over there, Sam,' Joan suggested, standing up, and her partner rose from the desk, nodding soberly.

Barely exceeding the five foot seven minimum height for male peace officers, Sam Cuchilo had the typical coppery brown, somewhat Mongoloid cast of features and thick-bodied, powerful build of a *Nemenuh** warrior. Dressed in a well-cut dark brown business suit, dark grey shirt and plain blue tie, he carried a .41 Magnum Smith & Wesson revolver with a four inch barrel in a Myers No. 4 cross draw holster at his left side. He could handle the heavy handgun with the dexterity displayed by his forefathers in the use of a bow and arrows, war-axe, lance, or firearms looted from the hated white brother during a war trail.

Joan Hilton was maybe three inches shorter than her partner. With her blonde hair done in a curly bubble-cut, she had a cheerful, good looking face. Her black trouser suit set off a buxom, firm-fleshed figure. She moved with a light-footed agility and there was a rubbery robustness about her that told of excellent physical condition. Women belonging to the criminal element of Gusher City warned new arrivals that Miss Hilton was one female badge who should always be treated with politeness and must not be crossed.

Picking up her Pete Ludwig shoulder bag – which held her identification wallet, handcuffs, snub-nosed Colt Cobra .38 Special revolver in a detachable holster, reserve ammunition and other items of official equipment, as well as a woman's usual articles – from the desk, she hooked its carry-strap over her left shoulder.

As Joan and Cuchilo walked towards the main entrance, the double doors opened to admit two more members of the Night Watch. Big, burly Deputy Sheriff Ian Grantley threw a grin at his tall, slender partner, Jake Melnick as they guessed what was happening.

*** Nemenuh: 'The People', the Comanche Indians' name for their nation.**

'Go on, grin your fool heads off!' Joan growled indignantly, knowing that she and Cuchilo would probably be kept busy with their investigation until long after the end of the watch. 'I just hope that you pair get caught as you're logging off.'

'I hope you get called out *after* you've logged off and are all tucked up, sleeping cosy, at home,' Cuchilo supplemented.

The Sheriff's Office worked a two-watch rota, from eight a.m. until four p.m. and four until midnight. If anything came up between midnight and eight, the deputies required to handle it would be called from their respective homes by the Gusher City Police Department's permanently-manned Business Office.

'Knowing me and Jake's luck,' answered the unabashed Grantley, 'that's real likely to happen.'

'Trust an Injun to think up the meanest way to get back at us, though,' Melnick went on. 'We should never have let them into our country.'

'Columbus was a rat-fink!' Cuchilo countered. 'It's his lousy navigation that's caused all the trouble. Us Indians were getting along just fine before he arrived.'

Despite the levity, Joan and Cuchilo wasted no time. Grantley and Melnick stood aside and allowed the other team to sign out in the Office Log. With that attended to, the blonde and her partner left the squadroom. They rode one of the elevators to the ground floor. Going out of a rear entrance, they crossed the official vehicles' parking lot to their black and white Oldsmobile Super 88 deputy car. Before they reached it, a black and white panel truck – its colours the reverse of their own – purred from the lot's gates and sped away.

'They must know which of us is driving,' Joan commented drily, nodding towards the departing Scientific Investigation Bureau's truck as her partner slid behind the Oldsmobile's steering wheel.

'If they had,' Cuchilo replied, 'they'd have waited and followed me, knowing how safe it would be.'

While her partner set the car into motion, Joan unhooked the radio's transmission microphone. She informed the dispatcher at Central Control of their departure and asked to be kept informed of any further developments.

'Do you know the victim, Joan?' Cuchilo inquired, sensing his partner's perturbation.

'I could do,' the blonde admitted, returning the microphone to its hook on the dashboard. 'I've friends all around that area. A lot of us bachelor girls live in Mockingbird Grove.'

'Say,' Cuchilo remarked, after a brief, uneasy silence. He wanted to divert Joan's thoughts from the possibility of the victim being a friend. 'Old Brad's getting to be a regular television personality.'

Joan smiled. That afternoon Deputy Sheriff Bradford Counter, of the Day Watch, had won the Rockabye County Department of Public Safety's Leatherslap, a combat shooting match, against some stiff opposition. Then he had been interviewed by the Gusher City television network's *Local View* programme that evening, taking part in a debate on the value of such competitions.

'He sure is,' the blonde agreed and threw a cold glare at the Comanche deputy. 'Now Alice won't be fit to know for a week. Why couldn't *you* have won that blasted Leatherslap?'

'Something told me you'd be getting around to *that*,' groaned Cuchilo. 'There's times I wish the town of Hell hadn't been closed down.* Then us *Kweharehnuh*† would still be holding out in the Palo Duro, instead of having to come in and smoke the peace pipe with you blasted palefaces.'

'I wish it, too,' Joan declared. 'Then maybe I'd've caught me a big, blond, handsome partner who gets to be seen on the television, instead of one who could only win a Leatherslap if they ran it on war-ponies and with bows and arrows.'

'If you was John Smith and I was Pocohantas, I'd have lit the fire,' Cuchilo sniffed. 'I just bet the last of the Mohicans didn't have my kind of troubles with Hawk-Eye either.

* Why and how the town was closed down is told in *Hell in the Palo Duro* and *Go Back to Hell*.

† Kweharehnuh: the Antelope band of the Comanche Nation.

Arguing briskly, as had become their way of relieving the tensions and apprehension which always arose when they were on their way to commence a homicide investigation, the deputies sped through the streets on the heels of the S.I.B.'s panel truck. There was little traffic and, without needing to augment their flashing red lights with the sirens, the peace officers soon reached the part of the city known as Mockingbird Grove.

All the trees in which mockingbirds had once congregated and nested had been cut down when the discovery of extensive oil deposits had caused Gusher City to expand its boundaries. In their place had grown a prosperous middle-rent community of small apartment buildings and private residences. It was, as Joan knew, normally a peaceful and law-abiding portion of the city.

Turning on to Dick Street, the deputies did not need to look at the numbers of the houses to know where they were to start their investigation. Already two black and white G.C.P.D. radio patrol cars, an all black Detective Bureau Ford sedan and an ambulance were parked along the edge of the right hand side-walk. Patrolmen held back the inevitable bunch of male and female onlookers who had gathered to see what was going on. On the drive, before the open door of Number Seventeen's garage, stood a Plymouth convertible with its top open and lights still on. Beyond the vehicle, a bulky male figure directed the beam of a flashlight at something on the ground.

A low sigh of relief broke from Joan as she decided that she did not know the victim.

Stopping the Oldsmobile behind the S.I.B. truck, Cuchilo remained in his seat while extracting his badge of office and hooking it on to his left buttonhole. Joan climbed straight out, swinging her bag on to her shoulder and walking around to join her partner as he emerged. Together, they strolled over to the truck.

'We'll help Terry to set up, Joan,' offered one of the three men who left the truck, indicating a second who had two cameras slung across his shoulders.

'Thanks, Morrie,' the blonde replied.

Before the deputies, or even the medical examiner could

approach the body, the photographer had to complete his work of recording the scene on film. Joan knew better than try to hurry that aspect of the investigation along. A thorough photographic record was invaluable, but getting it took time. So, leaving the two S.I.B. experts to assist the photographer, Joan and Cuchilo went past the truck, one of the r.p.'s and the D car. A patrolman holding a ballpoint pen and a loose-leaf notepad eyed them in a challenging manner.

'Woman Deputy Hilton, W-101,' Joan reported and indicated her partner. 'Deputy Sheriff Cuchilo, 958.'

' "Hilton" as in the hotel, ma'am?' the patrolman inquired noting the time of the deputies' arrival on the timetable he had been ordered to keep.

'I'm one of the poor side of the family,' the blonde explained and nodded to the big, bulky man who was approaching from the convertible. 'Hi, Denny.'

'Howdy, Joan, Sam,' greeted Sergeant Dennis O'Toole of the Lasher Division's Detective Squad. ' 'Tis a bad one.'

'They all are, one way or another,' Joan said quietly. 'What have we?'

Being the senior member of the deputy team, the blonde had to assume command of the investigation. Sam Cuchilo had accepted that from the beginning of their partnership, recognizing Joan's greater experience in all matters of practical law enforcement. From the prompt way in which O'Toole answered the question, he too felt no qualms about the possibility of having to take orders given by a woman.

'Victim's name is Amy Willer, thirty, unmarried, p.a. to a an exec. down at Euro-Tex,' the sergeant replied. 'Lived at home with her folks. Father's away on a fishing trip. Mother made the identification. She's in the house now. Got hysterical. One of our girls and the m.e.'s taking care of her.'

'Do we know what happened?' Cuchilo asked.

'Looks like she was robbed, her handbag's by her side, open. A r.p. saw the convertible standing like it is now, with the lights on. The shotgun went to check it out and found her. The top of her head's beaten to a pulp. And that's not just a figure of speech.'

'Nobody saw or heard anything?' Joan inquired.

'If they did, they haven't come forward to say so,' the sergeant replied. 'Which, in this kind of neighbourhood, they would've if they had.'

'That's for sure,' Joan agreed. 'They're not born cop-haters like down in the Bad Bit. Let's try asking around, anyway.'

Circulating amongst the onlookers, who lived in the surrounding houses, the deputies and O'Toole tried to obtain some clue that would throw a light on the reason for Amy Willer's death. It soon became obvious that nobody had seen or heard anything.

While the residents of Dick Street did not share the antipathy of dwellers in the slum area known as the Bad Bit where peace officers were concerned, they clearly did not mean to present their district in a bad light. So the citizens questioned by Joan, Cuchilo and the sergeant said much of the same thing. The victim had been a pleasant, respectable girl, devoted to her parents and without any known boy friends. Nobody could recollect having seen a car or any suspicious persons loitering in the vicinity of the Willers' house that evening.

'Which doesn't tell us a whole heap,' Cuchilo stated dryly as the deputies and O'Toole gathered by the Oldsmobile to compare notes.

'Most likely some of them would tell a different story about her if the interview was more private,' Joan replied. 'Maybe it won't come to that.'

If the victim had been murdered during the course of a robbery, there would be less reason for an extensive examination of her life and background; with the attendant possibility of digging up something derogatory to her memory as a further cause of grief to her parents.

The sudden blaze of light erupting from the photographer's camera told that he was still working. Floodlights glowed as the two S.I.B. experts commenced their preliminary examination of the surrounding area. From what the deputies could see, the convertible stood in the centre of a large square of concrete. It would be unlikely to produce any footprints, but would make the location of other scientific evidence so much easier.

'Let's go and see if Mrs. Willer can tell us anything,' Joan suggested, after studying the scene.

'Sure,' Cuchilo confirmed.

Going along the path, the deputies passed the convertible on the opposite side to where the body lay and reached the front door of the house without disturbing the cameraman. At Cuchilo's knock, the door was opened by a pretty young blonde policewoman. Relief flickered on the girl's face as Joan showed her id. wallet and introduced herself.

'The m.e.'s upstairs with Mrs. Willer,' the policewoman said, standing aside to let the deputies enter. 'I don't know if you'll be able to get anything from her tonight.'

'Has she said anything so far?' Joan inquired.

'Nothing much that made sense,' the policewoman admitted. 'She just kept repeating what a sweet, good, loving daughter Amy was and why would anybody want to hurt her? Then she kept asking for her husband.'

'I wonder if anybody knows where he's at?' Cuchilo remarked, half to himself.

'Catfishing along the Rio Grande, close to where Rockabye Creek flows in,' supplied the policewoman. 'I got that much out of her. Then, after the m.e. had taken over, I put in a call to your Euclid Sub-Office and asked if they could locate and bring him in.'

'Smart thinking,' Joan praised.

At that moment, the medical examiner came down the stairs.

'I've had to put Mrs. Willer under sedation,' he said. 'She was so hysterical that I couldn't do anything else.'

'Sure, doc,' Joan replied. 'Did she say anything?'

'Only something about having been afraid that Amy's gambling would land her in trouble,' the m.e. answered. 'I tried to find out what she meant, but she became so distraught that I had to quieten her down.'

'It can't be helped,' Joan said and looked at the policewoman. 'Come and help me look over the victim's room, if it's not locked.'

'I'll go and see if I can get started outside,' the m.e. commented and left by the front door.

Joan and the policewoman disappeared upstairs, leaving

Cuchilo in the hall. Ten minutes went by before the women returned.

'There wasn't anything to say where she'd been tonight,' Joan announced to her partner. 'But it looks as if she might have been off somewhere gambling.'

'Is that female intuition?' Cuchilo asked with a grin.

'Pure Sherlock Holmes-type deduction,' the blonde deputy corrected. 'There were three decks of cards and half a dozen dice in a drawer of her dressing-table. She'd a copy of *Scarne On Cards*, his book on dice, both of them had been read regularly, and maybe a dozen books of "certain" systems for winning at craps or poker. Taken with what her mother said to the m.e., I'm betting on her being a gal who liked to go gambling.'

'So she maybe went and came out a heavy winner tonight,' Cuchilo said thoughtfully. 'Was followed home and jumped for her winnings as she left the car to open the garage door.'

'It could be,' Joan agreed. 'Let's go and see if we can find Pinto Soyran around town, Sam.'

'Can't say's I know him,' the Comanche deputy declared.

'I do,' the blonde said grimly. 'He's a bad *hombre*. His caper is to hang around a game, follow the heavy winner home then jump him – or her – and take back the winnings.'

CHAPTER TWO

'Is this Soyran jasper in town?' Cuchilo asked.

'I don't know,' Joan admitted. 'If he is, he mostly holes up at a trap called the Blowing Wild down in the Bad Bit.'

While Cuchilo might not have heard of Pinto Soyran, he was fully conversant with the reputation of the bar in the Evans Park Division which went by the name of the Blowing Wild. It was not a place in which the peace officers could expect to find a spirit of cooperation from the owner or his customers.

'That's a choice address to be found dead in,' Cuchilo commented. 'And they say you can wind up that way just by breathing the air in it. Do we go check it out?'

'There's some who'd say we could do worse,' Joan replied.

'Anybody who'd say that must be an Indian-hater,' Cuchilo said dryly.

'They'd have *my* sympathy,' the blonde stated, eyeing her partner with mock disdain. 'Can you stay on here until her husband comes home, Velma?'

'Yo!' the policewoman agreed. 'I'll have to check with the house, though.'

'Go to it,' Joan said. 'If that heathen partner of mine was a gentleman, he'd open the door for us.'

'You gals are all for equality,' Cuchilo countered, going to obey. 'But, seeing that you outrank me, I'll have to do it.'

Presenting the women with a low bow that managed to appear full of unspoken offence, Cuchilo opened the door and followed them from the building. Outside all the levity left the deputies and they prepared to get down to business. The photographer had completed his work, but his big floodlights were still in use. While the m.e. bent over the victim's body, one of the S.I.B. men was dusting the car for fingerprints and the other stood looking at some small object. Going around the convertible, Joan and Cuchilo glanced at the slender, smartly-dressed figure which sprawled supine, its head a hideous and bloody mess pointing towards the door of the garage.

'What do you think, doc?' Joan asked, turning her gaze from the corpse. 'A guess at the time will do.'

'*Rigor mortis* hasn't set in yet,' the m.e. answered. 'This *is* just a guess, mind you, but I'd say not more than ninety minutes and not less than an hour.'

'Cause?' Joan went on almost automatically.

'So far I can see nothing to indicate other than death being caused by the injuries to the head. Whoever attacked her struck her more than one blow from the front. I'd say the first blow knocked her cold, but he kept hitting as she went down. She must have fallen against the car and it held her up until she was beaten down by the subsequent blows.'

'She must have opened the garage's door and been walking back to the car when the feller jumped her,' Cuchillo remarked, glancing at the smear of blood on the hood and down the side of the car. It suggested that the m.e. was correct in his assumption. 'Which brings up the point of why she didn't start yelling for help.'

'That's a point to think on,' Joan conceded and turned to the nearer of the S.I.B. men. 'Who did it, Morrie?'

Seen in his working clothes, Sergeant Morrie Lewtas had the build and appearance of a villain-type all-in wrestler. He was an expert police scientist, with an exceptionally keen pair of eyes that missed little when searching the scene of a crime.

'The man you want is five foot nine and three quarter inches, weighs one hundred and twenty-three pounds, four and two-thirds ounces. He's wearing Bermuda shorts, a buckskin shirt and clam diggers, walks with a limp and talks with a pronounced Deep South drawl, especially when he's committing a crime.'

'Don't all the baddies in the television shows these days?' Joan sniffed, unimpressed by Lewtas' words. 'What you mean is you don't know anything.'

'Put that way, yes, I don't know anything,' the sergeant agreed, then became serious. 'Not much anyway. It looks like robbery was the motive. Her handbag was open and the bill-fold's on the passenger seat. It's empty. According to her cheque book, she drew two thousand dollars out of her account this afternoon. From the look of her fingers, she'd been wearing a couple of rings but they'd been pulled off in a hurry. There's one strange thing, though. She's got Scarne's list of dice odds typed out and pasted into the flap of her handbag.'

'Seems like she was quite a gal for gambling,' commented Sergeant O'Toole, having come along the path in time to hear the last words. 'Feller just got me off to one side and claimed that she used to play the horses, with him putting the money down for her, pretty regular.'

'Was she lucky, or unlucky?' Cuchilo wanted to know.

'He *says* she was real lucky and they always finished ahead,' O'Toole replied. 'But I've never known a horse player who'd admit that he was a loser.'

'Do you know who they were betting with?' Joan asked.

'A local bookie. We know him and he's always been clean.'

'That doesn't mean too much,' Joan declared. 'She could be putting them down with more than one bookie.'

Neither Joan nor Cuchilo were surprised that the local detective would admit to knowing that a bookmaker was operating in his Division. As long as people insisted on gambling, the law enforcement officers preferred to have them do it through a known source. So, if the bookmaker followed an unwritten but accepted code of behaviour, he would be permitted to stay in business.

'You think she owed money and the bookie sent some muscle around to talk her into paying, huh Joan?' Lewtas inquired. 'I don't see it. They'd just throw a scare into her. Maybe they'd rough her up a mite, but they'd not go as far as killing her. That wouldn't get the bookie his money.'

'I'd say that all depends on who the bookie is,' Joan objected. 'The big money boys wouldn't let it get that far, because they hire well-trained help. But if she's been playing with some small operator, he'd have to take whatever muscle his bankroll would stand. Which means whoever he got wouldn't be too brainy or reliable. Most likely some cheap punk with all his brains in his fists, maybe flying high on pot or hard narcotics. That kind would forget what he was supposed to do, go hog-wild, start slugging and not know when to stop.'

'Everything points to it having been a robbery,' Lewtas commented. 'Which I'm not saying that the bookie's muscle wouldn't stop to clean her out after he'd finished slugging.'

'Who's her bookie, Denny?' Joan asked, turning to the local man.

'Name of Baxter. He's one of Jose Carrasco's boys and they can call on tophand help,' O'Toole answered. 'You want his address?'

'Can you go talk to him?' Joan requested. 'Sam and I want to follow up another lead.'

'I'll tend to it,' promised O'Toole.

'*Gracias*,' Joan drawled. 'Anything else, Morrie?'

'Only this,' Lewtas replied, holding out his right hand. 'It was on the ground by the car, near her feet. But I'm damned if I know whether it's connected with the killing.'

Gripped in the jaws of a forceps, 'this' proved to be a triangular piece of paper about four inches long and two deep. Moving it into the glow of the nearer floodlight, Lewtas allowed the deputies to take a closer look. Printed on the fragment in large black capital letters were the words 'LAM-BATT' and under them, somewhat smaller, 'IFORNIA 90038'. Below the letters on what would have been the right side of the sheet from which the fragment had been torn, was a small black triangular patch.

'Lam-Batt,' Joan repeated aloud. 'Does that mean anything to anybody?'

'Only that it came from California,' Cuchilo remarked, after the other men had given negative responses. 'I'd say it's part of an advertising brochure of some mind. The black patch is part of an illustration of the produce, whatever that might be.'

'From a gambling supply house, maybe,' Joan mused. 'See

what you scientifical wonders can learn from it for us, please Morrie.'

'Why do all you deputies try to sound like Buck Shields?' groaned Lewtas; referring to the First Deputy in charge of the Euclid Sub-Office, who invariably affected an attitude of distrust towards the 'scientifical wonders' of the S.I.B. 'I wouldn't mind it, but he's always the first to call us in on a case.'

'That's just so that he can introduce you city folks to the joys of country living,' Cuchilo grinned. 'There's times I think old Buck's running a real estate office on the side.'

'He is,' the second S.I.B. man put in, turning from the convertible. 'Sold me a hunting lodge with a leaking roof and direct access to the basement, through the kitchen floor. There are a few partials, but I'd be happier if we had this heap hauled in so we can do a thorough job.'

'That's your side of the case, Joan stated. 'We'll get going, Sam. Denny, have one of the r.p.'s stay on here.' She looked to where the policewoman was returning. 'Velma, see if you can get a couple of the neighbours to wait in the house with you.'

'Yo,' the girl replied, having notified her Divison's house that she would be staying at the scene of the crime. 'Is there anything else I can do?'

'Keep your ears open,' Joan answered. 'You might pick up something we haven't heard about the victim.'

Returning to the Oldsmobile, Cuchilo once more slid behind the steering wheel. With Joan reporting their intentions to Central Control, her partner started the car moving. They cruised at something higher than the speed limit across Lasher Division, through Jepson and entered Evans Park. There had been a gradual deterioration in the quality and condition of the property they had been passing since leaving Mockingbird Grove and from one of the most law abiding districts, they were heading into the most lawless area of the city.

The Blowing Wild bar was situated in Larch Street, a business and entertainment section of the Bad Bit. However, the street itself looked to be satisfactorily deserted as the

Oldsmobile swung on to it. Only one of the various premises showed signs of being open at such a late hour.

'Wouldn't it have to be the Blowing Wild?' Joan gritted.

'What would life be without its little challenges, paleface sister?' Cuchilo asked and his right hand dropped to unbutton his jacket.

'A damned sight easier,' Joan replied, taking up the microphone. 'S.O. 9 to Cen-Con.'

'Cen-Con by,' answered the Central Control dispatcher.

' "Code Six, Adam," Blowing Wild bar, Larch Street, Evans Park,' Joan said distinctly, so there could be no mistake in the receipt of her message. ' "Code One"?'

By using the police radio code, the blonde had informed the dispatcher that she and her partner would soon be leaving their vehicle to conduct an investigation. That much the dispatcher knew from the phrase 'Code Six'. Hearing the additional word 'Adam' told her that the crew of Sheriff's Office Unit Nine might require assistance. 'Code One' asked for confirmation that the message had been understood.

' "Code One",' repeated the dispatcher's contralto tones, agreeing that she had heard and understood the message. 'Will have nearest local car come to your location. Over and out.'

'Do we wait for the local heap?' Cuchilo asked.

'Let's go down and take a look who's inside first, then decide,' Joan replied. 'If Soyran's there, we don't want to spook him.'

Having no wish to warn the bar's occupants of their arrival, Cuchilo had halted the Oldsmobile about fifty yards away from the glow of light which was emanating from its window. On leaving the vehicle, Joan took certain precautions before setting off to reconnoitre the situation. Opening out the carrying strap, she made it so that she could hang it from her right shoulder, across her torso, to suspend the bag at her left hip. With it in position, she opened the fastener of the flap and nodded to her partner. Side by side, the deputies approached the bar's front door. Before they arrived, Cuchilo drew Joan's attention to the upper floor of the building. A glint of light showed through a narrow gap in the drapes of a window immediately above their destination.

'Could be he's rooming up there,' the blonde admitted. 'If he is, we'd best go in fast and throw down on him. Give him but half a chance and he'll start throwing lead.'

'We'd best not give him that chance then, paleface sister,' Cuchilo said grimly, right hand passing under his jacket to touch the magna stocks of his heavy calibre revolver. 'I hate folks throwing lead, especially in my direction.'

In passing, the deputies looked through the dirty ground floor window and took mental note of all they saw inside. The Blowing Wild bar was anything but fancy, or impressive, being a narrow, rectangular, poorly-lit room crammed between a cheap tailor's shop and a dingy, unhygienic-appearing drugstore. Nearly half of its area was taken up by a long counter. Behind this, a large, fat, surly man in his shirt sleeves was leaning and reading a copy of *Playboy* magazine. A line of narrow, high-backed booths stretched along the second wall, separated from the counter by a patch of bare, none-too-clean floor. Obviously the bar was a place for drinking and nothing else. It did not even offer its customers a juke box with which they could brighten the dull, uninspiring surroundings. Facing the front entrance, a door in the back wall gave access to the rear of the building.

Music came from inside the bar, despite the lack of a juke box. It originated from the rearmost booth, at the far side of which a couple of figures were necking with fierce intensity. They wore black leather jackets, but the length of both their hair made determination of their respective sexes impossible. Going by the motor cycle boot which emerged from the nearer side of the booth, another couple shared their companions' activities. A half empty whiskey bottle, four partially filled glasses and an ashtray heaped high with cigarette butts shared the table's top with a transistor radio.

Going by the window without stopping and attracting unwanted attention, the deputies reached the front door. Although Cuchilo opened it, he discarded further politeness and stepped inside first. Joan followed him towards the counter, deciding that she did not know the man behind it.

Although the bartender scowled at the deputies, his surly features showed no hint of recognition.

In the occupied booth, the couple separated from their clinch. They showed themselves to be a tall, well-built, sullenly handsome young man with shoulder long, mousey brown hair and a Zapata moustache and a pretty, shapely, brunette girl. Another long-haired male had, this time of rusty red and topping a beard, peered around the nearer end of the booth and a girl's blonde head appeared above it. Dull, hostile eyes glowered at the new arrivals. Either the young quartet guessed that Joan and Cuchilo were peace officers, or they merely disliked sharing the bar with other customers. Going by the rank stench of marijuana which came from the booth, it could have been either reason.

What might have been suspicion flickered across the bartender's unprepossessing face. From the angle at which the deputies approached him, he could gain no clue to their social status. Cuchilo had removed the deputy's badge from his buttonhole before leaving Dick Street and the Smith & Wesson was still in its holster, concealed beneath his jacket. Being slightly to her partner's rear, Joan's Pete Ludwig bag was hidden from the bartender's view by the Comanche deputy's stocky frame. She wondered if what she had taken for suspicion might amount to nothing more than a disinclination to start work. The bartender's opening words seemed to favour that theory.

'We don't serve liquor to Injuns,' the man said truculently, eyeing Cuchilo's dark brown face with its high cheekbones, somewhat aqualine nose and expressionless brown eyes.

'I stopped laughing at that kind of crack on the day I graduated from the Police Academy,' the Comanche deputy answered, suddenly looking more Comanche than deputy. 'And, what I've heard about it, I wouldn't wish the liquor you serve in this trap on to General Custer.'

'Cops, huh?' the bartender asked, darting a scowl at Joan's distinctive shoulder bag as she stepped alongside her partner.

'Deputies, both of us,' the blonde corrected and, as the man had raised his voice loud enough for his words to carry to the four customers in the booth, went on, 'If it'll save you shouting your head off, we'll go on over and show them our badges.'

'I dunno what you mean, blon—,' the bartender began and, seeing Joan's brow crease in an ominous frown, hurriedly revised his last word. 'Ma'am.'

'You got it right just in time,' Joan declared, noticing that the quartet had not resumed their necking but were watching and listening. 'Is Pinto around tonight?'

'Who?' asked the man behind the counter, darting a nervous glance at the rear door.

'Albert Ferdinand "Pinto" Soyran,' the blonde elaborated coldly. 'Black hair, brown eyes, scar on his chin. Six foot one, one hundred and eighty pounds – Do I need to go on with it?'

'Oh, *that* Pinto!' the bartender ejaculated, straightening up. 'I'll just go and—'

'Why we'd just hate for you to take all that trouble on our account,' Joan answered. 'Stay put and enjoy the nudie pictures. We know *all* about that button at the other end of the counter. Seeing you've been so helpful, I'll press it for you before we go upstairs. Watch him, Sam.'

'He's watched,' Cuchilo stated and, seeing the man tense as if to carry out his intention of moving, leaned on the counter. 'Stay put, white brother. Wise old saying of my people, "Man who stays in his lodge doesn't get scalped outside it." '

For a few seconds the bartender stood undecided as to what he should do. He had orders to press the button of the alarm bell in the event of peace officers arriving with the intention of going upstairs. However, doing it under the prevailing conditions would not be easy. Cuchilo's eyes were fixed on the fat face as if seeking to read the bartender's every thought. More than that, the deputy's features had all the savage menace of a *Kweharehnuh* brave-heart hoping to count coup on an enemy. The bartender had weight and size on his side, but something told him that he might regret any attempt to take advantage of it against the stocky, unsmiling Comanche deputy. Throwing another look at the rear door, the bartender gave a resigned shrug.

'I was only trying to help,' he said sullenly.

'We do dearly admire to meet an obliging member of the public,' Cuchilo replied. 'and we thank you for thinking about us.'

Satisfied that her partner could keep the bartender under control, Joan strolled towards the rear end of the counter. Looking down, she saw where the alarm bell's wire emerged. She followed it with her eyes as it ran along the bottom of the wall and around to the back door. Deciding the easiest point to cut the wire would be at the door, she turned in that direction.

Slipping out from between the table and the back wall, the moustached young man stepped in front of Joan. His leather jacket was open, exposing a dirty white tee-shirt tucked into Levi's pants. Placing his hands on his hips, he leered at the blonde deputy in a defiant manner. Cursing softly, the other man tried to extricate himself from the narrow space between the seat and the table. Grins twisted the lips of the girls.

'Go, Ape-Boy, go!' hissed the brunette.

'You got something in mind, pantie-fuzz?' the moustached young man demanded, his speech showing that he had taken too many drinks.

'Nothing that concerns you,' Joan replied. 'So stop flexing your muscles and go sit down like a good little boy.'

'You watch the mouth, pantie-fuzz,' advised the second man, still not clear of the table. 'Old Ape-Boy don't like the smell of pig-fuzz.'

'He'll be smelling more of them if he doesn't sit down,' Joan warned, without halting or changing pace.

'Who's going to make me sit down, pantie-fuzz?' Ape-Boy challenged, teetering slightly on his heels. 'You figure you and Sitting Bull there can do it? Shug and me don't have a piece, or a blade on us, so it'd have to be with bare hands. You going to be *loco* enough to try it, pantie-fuzz?'

Cuchilo let out a low grunt of anger. Although he had intended to keep the bartender under observation until Joan had cut the bell's wire, he was compelled to change his mind. Swinging from the counter, he prepared to go to his partner's assistance.

'Sonny,' Joan said quietly, going closer to Ape-Boy and measuring the distance with her eyes. 'If you don't go back and sit down, I'm fixing to go right over you. That's not a threat, it's a promise.'

CHAPTER THREE

'WATCH Sitting Bull, Shug boy,' the moustached young man ordered, still standing on spread apart feet and with arms akimbo. 'Go to it, pantie-fuzz. You just lay the knuckles on m—'

Joan had already figured out that she would have to do as Ape-Boy asked. Primed by marijuana and whiskey, he would not be amenable to verbal reasoning. Nor would drawing her gun offer any solution. In his present state of mind, Ape-Boy was unlikely to respond sensibly to the Colt Cobra's threat. Every instinct she possessed warned Joan that she would have to use the gun if she produced it. Even if she did no more than inflict a flesh wound on the young man, the very 'liberal' *Gusher City Mirror* would be only too eager to run a story about how a trigger-happy peace officer had shot an unarmed 'boy' without any justification. Wanting to avoid stirring up the kind of distorted story and resultant smear campaign which the 'liberal' newspaper did so well, she had decided on her line of action.

Letting out a well-simulated hiss of anger, Joan swung her right arm with the hand open as if for a slap. Seeing the amateurish-looking way she acted, Ape-Boy grinned and moved his head back. Cold sober, he would have known better; but the liquor and narcotics had done their work too well for him to realize the danger. In removing his head, he thrust forward his stomach. Instantly Joan's right hand halted in its swing. Moving closer in anything but an amateurish fashion, the blonde pivoted slightly and threw all her weight behind her knotted left fist. Hurled with speed, power and precision, an almost classical hook brought her knuckles into contact with his offered solar plexus. Caught with such unexpected force, Ape-Boy belched out all the air from his lungs. He stumbled back a couple of paces and folded over. Nor did his troubles end there.

Following up her advantage with equal speed, Joan dug both hands into Ape-Boy's hair and jerked downwards. Working in perfect coordination, her right leg bent and rocketed up from the floor. Driven by powerful calf and thigh muscles, her knee smashed against the centre of the moustached face. The impact caused Ape Boy's torso to change direction once more. Flung erect, blood gushing from his nostrils and his skull seeming to be exploding with shattering agony, he might have counted himself fortunate that Joan had released his hair on kneeing him. The force with which he was lifted erect and pitched backwards would have seen a lump of his scalp left in the blonde's hands. Crashing into the wall at the hinged side of the door, he slid glassy-eyed and limply to the floor.

Fully confident in Ape-Boy's toughness, Shug had been unable to imagine that anything could go wrong. So he had concentrated his main attention on the advancing male deputy. When things went wrong for Ape-Boy, Shug found himself faced with a problem and vacillating as he tried to decide which of the peace officers posed the greater threat.

As she swung around from dealing with Ape-Boy, Joan saw Cuchilo coming to her assistance and noticed something else. Taking advantage of the distraction, the bartender had forsaken the 'nudie' pictures in *Playboy* and was moving along the counter in the direction of the alarm bell's button.

'Watch the barkeep, Sam!' Joan snapped and moved to solve Shug's dilemma, although certainly not in a manner which would have met with his approval.

Catching the bearded man's right shoulder in her right hand, Joan gave a sharp tug which spun him around in a full circle. As he returned to face her, she whipped her left fist upwards and across. With the deadly accuracy a trained boxer could not have bettered, she landed a savage punch to the edge of Shug's jaw. His head snapped sideways and, twirling again on awkward, uncontrolled feet, he sprawled belly down on to the booth's table. Its legs buckled under his weight. Collapsing, with the whiskey bottles, glasses, ashtray and radio cascading around Shug's flaccid body, the top of the table effectively trapped the two girls' legs as they tried to get out and avenge the assaults on their escorts.

Turning at Joan's yell, Cuchilo darted to intercept the bartender. With a ringing *Kweharehnuh* war whoop – a sound dreaded by Texans long after the other bands of the Comanche nation had made peace and quit the war trail* – the deputy slapped his right hand on to the top of the counter. Swinging up his legs, he vaulted over with the ease his forefathers had shown when bounding afork a war pony. Sliding across the counter, he hurled both feet into the man's chest. Taken by surprise, the bartender was caused to retreat almost to his original position. Spitting out curses, he snatched a bottle from the shelf fixed to the side wall.

'I'll fix you, you Injun bastard!' the bartender shouted, smashing the bottle and rushing forward.

Cuchilo studied the situation with considerable speed, deciding that the sharp spikes of glass would be directed at his face. There was no room for him to try to side step the attack, but he did not let that worry him. Waiting until the jagged remains of the bottle thrust towards him, he shoved back with his left foot and twisted his torso to the left. His right fist, with the knuckles outwards, raised until it was in front of his left shoulder and the bent left arm was tucked tight against his side with its hand open, fingers extended together and thumb bent across the upturned palm. It was a fighting stance which had never been known by his free-ranging ancestors.

Around snapped Cuchilo's right arm, the back of his fist cracking against the forward-driving wrist and deflecting the broken bottle before it reached his face. With the danger of being cut reduced, the deputy stabbed out his left hand. The extended fingers ploughed viciously into the bartender's solar plexus. To the recipient of the blow, it seemed that he had run into the blunted head of a war lance and that the missile would continue until it exploded out of his back. A strangled, agonized squawk burst from the man's lips. Letting the bottle fall from his fingers, he retreated and clutched

* Why the Kweharehnuh did not make peace at the same time as the other bands is told in *Sidewinder*.

at the stricken region with both hands. Unfortunately for him, he did not go back far enough.

Opening his right hand, to adopt the same position and style as the left, Cuchilo struck again. Swinging both hands up and down, he chopped their heels into the sides of the bartender's flabby neck. Gagging and croaking in pain, barely able to breathe and replenish his forcibly emptied lungs, the man dropped to his knees.

'Make peace, white brother,' the deputy advised. 'Grandfather Cuchilo used to tell me that a Comanche boy who always obeyed his father, respected the tribal laws and thought good, clean thoughts would come to no harm. Just to make sure he was right, I got up to black belt at judo and karate in college.'

Listening to her partner's little speech, Joan could not hold back a grin. As she prepared to cross and quieten down the two screeching, cursing girls, she became aware of footsteps beyond, and approaching, the rear door. So she ignored the girls, seeing that they had not managed to free themselves from the table. Darting to the wall, she flattened herself against it on the opposite side of the door to where Ape-Boy was lying. Her right hand flashed into the mouth of the shoulder bag, emerging with the Colt Cobra gripped ready for use. The door was jerked open and a short, slender, rat-faced man came through.

'Fred says for you to hold the noise do—' he began.

The words ended abruptly as he stared at the booth, with Shug still sprawled on the broken table and the girls trying to free themselves from under it. From there, his gaze swung to the bar. Hearing the newcomer enter, Cuchilo had turned. The deputy rested both elbows on top of the counter, using a double-handed hold to line the Smith & Wesson 'maggie' he had drawn while turning. Despite the threat of the heavy calibre revolver, the man made a motion as if to swing around and leave the room.

'Don't try it!' Joan hissed, stepping behind the newcomer and thrusting the muzzle of her Cobra against his spinal column. 'And if you raise your voice, I'll bust your head.'

'Wha – Who—?' croaked the man, standing as if turned to stone.

At that moment the front door opened. A tall, heavily built man wearing a sports jacket and flannel slacks entered, followed by two G.C.P.D. patrolmen and a big, black haired, buxom woman who, apart from the Pete Ludwig bag on her left shoulder, might have been a local housewife come to see what all the excitement was about.

'Hi, Joan,' the woman greeted. 'The U.S. Cavalry's arrived.'

'With perfect timing,' the blonde answered. 'See to things down here, Rachel. Come with Sam and me, Dave.'

'Yo!' Sergeant Dave Bulpin gave the time-honoured cavalry assent.

'There's a feller behind here, boys,' Cuchilo remarked as he rose and vaulted back over the bar. 'He's not looking too good.'

'There looks to be a lot of *that* going around,' commented one of the patrolmen dryly, looking from the moaning, feebly moving Ape-Boy to the motionless Shug. 'And it's contagious.'

Leaving Sergeant Rachel Winters – whose reputation as a tough, stand-no-nonsense peace officer almost equalled Joan's – and the two patrolmen to take charge of the room's occupants, the deputies and Bulpin went swiftly, but quietly, upstairs. Behind them, silence fell on the room. Newly arrived in Gusher City, the two girls had not recognized Joan. They had been in the Evans Park district for long enough to have had Rachel pointed out to them and her reputation explained. So they knew better than continue creating a disturbance. Joan was pleased about that. While she no longer expected to find Pinto Soyran on the premises, there was somebody upstairs. Whoever it was clearly had no wish to attract attention to the bar. That suggested something of an illicit nature was going on. An unexpected entrance by her party would be the safest way of avoiding trouble.

On reaching the first floor landing, Joan turned towards the front of the building. A gleam of light glowed through the crack beneath one of the doors, but she and her companions did not go there immediately. Instead, they produced and fixed their badges in plain sight. Then they moved silently forward. Seeing the deputies both held revolvers, Bulpin drew a Browning Hi-Power 9mm automatic from its shoulder holster under his left arm.

'Let's go in!' Joan breathed.

Raising his left leg, the big detective kicked open the door. Plunging into the room and fanning out fast, the three peace officers lined their weapons at the nine men who were seated around the table playing poker.

'Peace officers here!' Joan snapped, while Cuchilo and Bulpin looked around the room to see if it had other occupants. 'This is a raid.'

The words were those which Sheriff Jack Tragg and Chief of Police Phineas Hagen had selected as the best challenge for use in such a situation. Not only were the trio displaying their badges openly, but Joan had announced their identity in a manner which avoided confusion. Nothing she had said could possibly be misconstrued by the men hearing it.

Startled exclamations had risen and chairs were shoved back as the men began to get to their feet. Eight of the nine, who had all removed their jackets, looked like reasonably prosperous, law-abiding citizens. The ninth, behind a large box containing decks of cards, stacks of chips and a pile of money, was tall, lean, with the pallor that had long been the trademark of a professional gambler. Studying the faces in the light of the single lamp hanging over the table, Joan failed to locate Pinto Soyran.

'Who's banking the game?' Joan inquired.

'I am,' the pallid man answered.

'What's this all about, officers?' asked a plump jovial-featured player to the right of the banker.

'We'll explain downstairs,' Joan replied. 'Move out.'

'Now just a dog-blasted minute!' barked a burly man angrily. 'We're only having a friendly game—'

'I don't doubt it,' Joan replied. 'So we'll go downstairs and talk.'

'We'd better do it, boys,' suggested the plump man. 'Can we put our money away, officer?'

'Just what's lying before you,' Joan decided. 'We'll lock the rest, chips, bank, pot and cards in here as evidence.'

'Yeah?' growled the burly player. 'I've heard all about cops doing that—'

'Well, as to that, I've faith in the honesty of our local officers,' the chubby man interrupted. 'So I'm willing to do as they say.'

Following the speaker's example, the other players pocketed their money. Then they trooped by the peace officers towards the door. Letting them go by, Joan spoke quietly.

'Oh, Fred.'

'Yes—?' the plump man said, starting to turn Joan's way before realizing his error.

'He's the one we want, Dave,' the blonde stated. 'You can have the banker and those yacks downstairs. Do what you want about the players.'

All the men had come to a halt and swung around, puzzled by the latest development. Then the players stared at the burly detective, waiting to hear what their fate was going to be.

'You fellers cash in your chips, split the last pot and go home,' Bulpin ordered, then glanced at the deputies. 'Taking them in on 631's* just loses us sleeping time. I like to go to bed when I log off watch, not sit around court all day waiting to give evidence.'

Mutters of relief broke from the players at learning that they would be allowed to retain their money and avoid prosecution. Returning their weapons to holsters, Cuchilo and Bulpin went to supervise the cashing in of the chips.

'Not you, Fred,' Joan said chidingly as the plump man started to move towards the table.

'May I ask why I'm being singled out for different treatment?

'Because you're not a player. You're the floorwalker for the game.'

In addition to the banker and other employees, most organized gambling games had a floorwalker present. Posing as an ordinary player, he surpervised the whole affair. In ad-

* Texas Penal Code (Offences Against Public Property and Economy Section) Article 631; Knowingly Entering A Gambling House. Penalty fine not exceeding $50.00.

dition to making sure that the bank received its fair cut of each pot, he would also – as Fred had done – try to prevent trouble in case of a raid. If there should be a raid, he hoped to remain unsuspected and be released with the other players. Then he could set about arranging legal assistance for the arrested employees and attending to other matters.

Unfortunately for Fred, Joan was fully conversant with such details and had been in possession of a clue to his identity unwittingly supplied by the man who had carried his message down to the barroom.

'I still don't kn—' Fred commenced, watching the other players collecting their property.

'Don't bug me, for God's sake!' Joan warned. 'I know who you are and why you're here. Only I'm after something a damned sight more important than any penny ante poker game.'

'It might not be the biggest game in town, but it's not penny ante!' Fred corrected, indignant at the suggestion that he was running a low stake game. Then he peered at Joan's badge. 'Hey! You're not with the blue-noses,* that's a deputy's badge. I didn't think that gambling came under your jurisdiction.'

'Not usually,' agreed Joan. 'But it could easily get that way with those two yacks you've got on guard downstairs.'

'Henry and his buddy?' the floorwalker said, raising his eyebrows. 'Why, what did they do?'

'Tried to jump me when they saw I was coming up here,' Joan explained.

'They did that?' Fred yelped angrily, alarm showing on his face. 'God blast those stupid sons-of-bitches. They were told that they hadn't got to try to muscle the law.'

'The lesson hadn't sunk all the way in,' Joan said dryly. 'Could be it will have, time they come out of The Walls.'

Fred's face showed even greater alarm at the blonde's reference to 'The Walls', the State Penitentiary at Huntsville. While the two young men might not be sent there, a charge of assaulting peace officers would carry a stiff penalty. His organization would not be pleased with the attendant pub-

*** Bluenoses: Vice & Gambling Detail of the Gusher City Police Department.**

licity and the possibility of a tight clamp down all gambling as a result of the pair's behaviour. There was also another, more personal consideration for him to bear in mind.

'Hey now, Miss—' the floorwalker said hurriedly, 'I told them—'

'You should have made sure that they listened and understood,' Joan replied unsympathetically. 'Anyways, what are a couple of pot-headed punks like them to you?'

'Henry's my wife's sister's kid,' Fred admitted sadly. 'If she hears that – Hell, I never thought anything—'

'So?'

'So you're looking for something. Maybe I can help you find it.'

'How?'

'Not until we can talk in private,' Fred protested, with a pointed glance at the banker.

'In the hall,' Joan suggested. 'Unless any of the other rooms are in use.'

'If they are,' Fred growled, 'I'll make that fat slob downstairs wish he'd never been born.'

Taking Fred into the hall, away from the head of the stairs, Joan asked, 'Was Pinto Soyran in tonight, Fred?'

'That crud?' the floorwalker snorted. 'He'll not show his face around one of our games.'

'You're levelling?'

'You know his bag. Let that start happening and there's damned soon a squeal that turns on the heat. No sir, Miss. Pinto Soyran knows better than come around any of our games.'

'Who's been playing tonight?'

'The guys you saw in there. Three, four others earlier. I don't know any of their names.'

'Any women?' Joan asked.

'Naw!' Fred sniffed. I only know one woman around town who comes to poker games, but I've not seen her tonight.'

'Who is she?' Joan demanded. 'And don't hit me with that "I don't know" jazz.'

'A gal called Miller, or some such. Not much of a looker, but she can sure play a mean hand of stud or draw.'

'Does she play often?'

'Two, three times a month at one game or another, from what I've heard. Say! What's happened to her?'

'Should anything have happened to her?' Joan countered.

'Lady, I wasn't born yesterday,' Fred pointed out. 'When two deputies raid a game, then start asking about a particular player *and* a certain party, something bad's happened.'

'She was robbed and killed outside her home,' Joan told him. 'Likely after she'd been out gambling.'

'And it looks like a Pinto Soyran caper?'

'The m.o.'s pretty close,' Joan admitted. 'Except that he's never washed out a victim before.'

'It was only a matter of time before he did,' Fred said soberly. 'Only, as far as I know, he's not in town. The word'd've been passed if he was.'

'He could have just come back tonight,' Joan replied. 'This's his hang out when he's in town. Way the bartender acted when we came in and asked about him, we thought he was up here and came to look.'

'So *that's* how you got on to us,' Fred ejaculated, sounding relieved. 'We only moved into this trap a few days back and the old owner didn't say anything about it being Pinto's hang out. Anyways, the Miller dame didn't show at the game here tonight.'

'Nothing I've heard's making me think twice about charging Henry,' the blonde warned.

'Maybe I could find out where she was at for you?' Fred suggested. 'The organization likes us to play square with the law here. If you drop me off at my place, I'll call you in the morning—'

'If there's one thing we're long on at the Sheriff's Office, it's telephones,' Joan interrupted. 'You can call from there and I want the answer *tonight*. If I get it, Henry and his buddy can go tomorrow without a stain on their characters. And do I mean *go*. Don't let them stop until they're miles from Rockabye County.'

CHAPTER FOUR

'CEN-CON to S.O. Nine!' crackled the dispatcher's voice over the Oldsmobile's radio.

'S.O. Nine by,' Joan Hilton answered into the microphone. 'We are just leaving Dick Street—'

'Have you another destination?' interrupted the dispatcher.

'Negative,' Joan admitted, glancing at her partner.

The time was nine thirty on Tuesday morning. Neither of the Oldsmobile's occupants had had more than a couple of hours sleep the previous night. From the way the conversation with the dispatcher was going, they figured that their chances of logging off and going home had diminished for some reason.

To prevent the poker game's banker from becoming suspicious and ensure Fred's full cooperation, Joan had changed her plans at the Blowing Wild. Instead of taking the floorwalker with her and leaving the others to be dealt with by Sergeant Bulpin, she had had them all delivered to the Department of Public Safety Building. Once there she had escorted Fred to the Sheriff's Office, on the pretence of allowing him to call a lawyer while his companions were placed in the cells.

Leaving Cuchilo to supervise Fred during the floorwalker's attempts to obtain information about the dead girl, Joan had reported to First Deputy Alvarez in the Watch Commander's office. She had told her superior all that had happened since she had left to start the investigation and of the bargain she had struck with the floorwalker. On the latter matter, Alvarez had given his approval and agreement. Charging the two men with attempted assault could be tricky and was, in Joan's opinion, a waste of time. Alvarez agreed and had remarked that, if he knew Joan, they had agreed and been sufficiently punished for their stupidity. So they would spend the night in the cells, then be released in the morning with orders to get the hell out of Rockabye County.

Despite Fred's comments on the subject, Joan had requested that an all points bulletin be circulated in the county for Pinto Soyran to be picked up and brought in for questioning. She also wanted a call for information to be passed to the Identification & Criminal Records Division of the Texas Department of Public Safety at Austin. Receiving up-to-date information from every law enforcement agency in the State, I.C.R. could probably locate Soyran and would also supply details of other criminals who used a similar method of operation.

Although Alvarez had agreed to do as Joan asked, he had warned that the theory concerning the killer having followed the girl home from a game could be wrong. On bringing the convertible to the D.P.S. Building for a more thorough examination than was possible at the scene of the crime, the S.I.B. team had made a significant discovery. They had found an envelope with just under nineteen thousand dollars in it concealed under the floor mat of the front passenger seat. If the killer had been at the game and followed the girl with the intention of robbing her of the winnings, it seemed likely that he would have made a more determined effort to find it.

Joan could not argue with that point and, having organized her requests, Alvarez had given her other information. The search of the car had only produced one other item; a golden four-leaf clover broken from a charm bracelet. That it had belonged to the dead girl had been confirmed by her father. Mr. Willer had been brought home by a deputy from the Euclid Sub-Office, arriving shortly after Joan had put in her 'Code Six, Adam' call. So Alvarez had spoken to him on the telephone. Although distressed, Willer had managed to supply some information. As the deputies had suspected, Amy had been a compulsive gambler. The fact that she had been wearing her golden charm bracelet had told that she had gone to a game of some kind; she never wore it unless meaning to gamble and it was not in its usual place in her dressing table. She had also been wearing two fairly valuable diamond rings. Her father had not, however, been able to suggest where she might have gone that night.

Deciding to leave a more lengthy interview with the parents until the next day, Joan had heard other reports. Sergeant O'Toole had visited Amy's bookie and been told that she was a lucky horse-player who had never failed to settle her account immediately when she lost. That appeared to rule out the possibility of her death having been caused by her welshing on her debts.

There had only been one more piece of information. The source of the fragment of paper had been traced. A check had shown that California 90038 was the postal code for Hollywood. So Alvarez had called the police there on the telephone and they had supplied the answer. 'Lam-Batt' could only be one thing, a company called 'Glam-Batt' which produced and sold girl fight photographs, movies, cartoon folders and booklets. Although the company's sole address was a post office box number, the Hollywood police had promised to have an officer waiting to interview whoever came to open the box and find out if they had customers in or around Rockabye County.

That had been when Cuchilo made his appearance, bringing news which had prevented himself and his partner from calling it a day and logging off watch. First calling a senior member of his organization, Fred had explained the situation and was told to demand full cooperation from the other floorwalkers. That had not unduly surprised the listening Cuchilo. Having spent considerable money on setting up the various games in Gusher City and around the county, they had no wish for trouble with the law. The situation with the gambling games parallelled that of the bookies as far as the law enforcement agencies were concerned. Their acceptance of the correctly-run, honest games had paid a dividend. On his fourth call, Fred had discovered where Amy had been playing that night. She had been at a high stake game in Leander Division. Although she had sat in at eight and left shortly before ten, she had taken away close to twenty thousand dollars. She had warned the other players that she could not stay after ten, so there had been no complaints when she cashed in her chips.

Not all that information had been passed over the telephone. Obtaining the Leander floorwalker's address from Fred, Joan and Cuchilo had paid him a visit and conducted a more lengthy interview. They had learned the names of the other players, but the floorwalker insisted that none of them had left the game shortly after Amy had taken her departure.

By the time the deputies had returned to the D.P.S. Building, it had been far too late for them to bother going home. So Joan had slept on a camp bed in the Watch Commander's office, while Cuchilo and Alvarez used similar accommodation in the squadroom.

That morning, after washing up and tidying their appearances in the male and female locker rooms, Joan and Cuchilo had eaten breakfast at the Badge Diner; a favourite haunt of peace officers from the D.P.S. Building. Back at the Office, they had asked the Records and Information Bureau to suggest the names of muggers, especially any favouring a m.o. similar to that used by the killer. With that done, they had set off to carry out the most unpleasant task of any homicide investigation, questioning the victim's next-of-kin.

Although Mr. and Mrs. Willer had been somewhat more composed, they had been unable to offer a motive, other than that she had been killed during a robbery, for their daughter's death. Amy had always been a quiet girl who avoided close friendships and her sole interest had been gambling. As far as her parents knew, she had no enemies, nor had she acted in a worried or alarmed manner in the days immediately before her death. One fact had emerged under Joan's tactful questioning. Usually Amy would have returned from the game at a much later hour. However, she was to have gone on vacation that morning and, having to make an early start, she had decided not to stay out late. That reduced the chances of the murderer knowing her habits and having waited to rob her on her return. Beyond furnishing a more detailed description of the missing items of jewellery, the Willers had been unable to give further information.

Giving the grieving couple what small comfort they could, the deputies had left the house. It had been their intention to contact the Sheriff's Office and ask if any reports had come in for them. If they received a negative answer, or the information was not urgent, they meant to visit the Euro-Tex Clothing Company and question Amy's work-mates to see what could be learned. As they had recently brought to a successful conclusion a case which had saved Euro-Tex a large sum of money,* they figured that the company would be cooperative. Cuchilo had hardly started the Oldsmobile moving before the radio had crackled into life with their call sign.

'Go to Forty-Six, Mockingbird Crescent,' the dispatcher ordered. 'Reported "woman down". Injuries of similar nature to those of victim in your current investigation. "Code One"?'.

' "Code One",' Joan confirmed. 'Any further details, Cen-Con?'

'Negative,' the dispatcher answered. 'S.O. Twelve already sent to scene.'

'We're on our way,' Joan said. 'Over and out.'

'Less than a mile from here,' Cuchilo commented as Joan returned the microphone to its hook. 'Could he have hit twice?'

'He's a cool son-of-a-bitch if he did,' Joan replied. 'Leaving the Willer girl in plain view like that, he ought to have expected her to be found pretty quickly. Once that happened, the area would soon be swarming with badges.'

'He might have hit the other girl first,' Cuchilo pointed out. 'She must have been hidden, or she'd have been found sooner.'

In most respects, the scene on Mockingbird Crescent resembled that at Dick Street the previous night. It was a similar, if slightly higher-rent, kind of residential area, pleasant and homely in the morning sun. The specialists' vehicles had already arrived and patrolmen controlled the invariable groups of kibitzers. A gravel driveway ran from

* Told in *The Owlhoot.*

the sidewalk and disappeared beyond the end of the house before which the official vehicles were parked.

There was one difference from the Willer killing. A Sheriff's Office Oldsmobile was already on the scene.

Halting their car behind the other deputies' vehicle, Cuchilo looked around. He had no difficulty in locating Deputy Sheriff Bradford Counter who was standing talking to two women on the opposite sidewalk.

With a height of six foot three and the muscular development of a 'Mr. Universe', topped by curly golden blond hair and an almost classically handsome face, Brad Counter tended to stand out even in a Texas crowd. He wore a genuine Harris tweed sports jacket, dark blue sharkskin shirt with a dark green silk cravat tucked into its open neck, dark grey flannel slacks and Sears-Roebuck crepe-soled kangaroo hide boots. He looked more like a high-income business executive, dressed informally on a day off, than a peace officer. Nothing about the excellently tailored sports jacket as much as hinted that its left side hung over a .45 Colt Government Model automatic pistol in a Hardy-Cooper spring shoulder holster.

Cuchilo knew that the weapon was there and how Brad could handle it with deadly speed and accuracy should the need arise. In fact, the Comanche deputy was willing to admit that the big blond was the best all round gun-handler in the Sheriff's Office. Such a talent was an asset in the jet-age just as it had been in the four decades following the War Between The States, when a peace officer's speed on the draw was often the only means of maintaining law and order. Yet there was more to Brad than expensive clothing and exceptional ability is using firearms.

The blond giant had enormous physical strength, backed by a thorough knowledge of self defence and unarmed combat. He was also an efficient member of the Sheriff's Office. Cuchilo had often wondered how many of these traits had been inherited from Brad's paternal great-grandfather. In the turbulent 1860's, '70's and '80's, Mark Counter had earned himself a name for considerable proficiency in all those lines;* as well as for being a better than fair hand with the ladies.

* Mark Counter's story is told in the author's Floating Outfit books.

No matter in what way Brad had come by his qualities, there had been no arguments from the other deputies when Sheriff Tragg had selected him to represent his department in the Leatherslap the previous afternoon.

There had been a time, not too long back, when the other members of the Sheriff's Office would not have been so confident. In those days, Brad had been a rookie. In some opinions, he was not even that. Unlike the rest of the deputies, he had come into the Sheriff's Office – an honour graduate of the University of Southern Texas' Police Science and Administration class and having qualified on the Federal Bureau of Investigation's exacting police officers' training course – without having passed through the G.C.P.D.'s Training Academy, or spending as much as one day at practical law enforcing in the capacity of patrolman or city detective.

Numerous predictions of Brad's failure had been made. It had even been hinted that Jack Tragg had taken him on as a means of winning approbation and reciprocal favours from the very wealthy Counter family. That had not been the case. After examining the blond's record at U.S.T. and reading the reports of his F.B.I. instructors, the sheriff had decided that he possessed a natural aptitude for the deductive side of law enforcement. The appointment had been an experiment; and a successful one.

Guided in his early days by Deputy Sheriff Tom Cord, Brad had developed fast. When bushwhack lead had cut Cord down, the blond giant had teamed up with his late partner's niece to hunt the killers.* With Tom Cord's murder avenged, Brad had continued to work with Woman Deputy Alice Fayde. They functioned together as a smoothly co-ordinated team and had cracked their share of tough cases.

Before Cuchilo could leave the car and join Brad, the blond giant's partner appeared from between the S.I.B.'s truck and the ambulance. Raising a hand in greeting, she walked towards the Oldsmobile.

On any busy street in a city, it would have been possible to find a few more beautiful and shapely women than Alice

* Told in *The Professional Killers*.

Fayde. There would also be a large number who were far less attractive and well endowed. Five foot seven in height, with red hair cropped short and curly since her return from a hectic vacation in Mexico,* she had good looking – if not ravingly beautiful – features which showed strength of will, self-possession and intelligence in their lines. Dressed in a stylish grey two-piece and plain dark blue blouse, she displayed a thirty-seven, twenty-five, thirty-five inch figure without blatantly flaunting it. Everything about her hinted at cool, efficient, self-reliant confidence.

'We caught it, Joan, Sam,' Alice greeted in an attractive Texas drawl, as the deputies alighted and joined her on the street. 'But we figured you'd best come on over and take a look.'

Neither Joan nor Cuchilo saw the words as an attempt to evade the responsibility of investigating a homicide. Since joining the Sheriff's Office, Alice had never shirked her share of the work-load.

Starting as a uniformed policewoman, Alice had risen swiftly through the ranks of the Bureau of Women Officers. From serving as a detective in such diverse Divisions as Upton Heights and Evans Park – the opposite ends of Gusher City's social scale – she had progressed through some of the G.C.P.D.'s specialist Bureaus to win one of two coveted appointments to the Sheriff's office. Not as the normal kind of woman deputy, operating a switchboard, handling female prisoners, or performing routine secretarial duties, but to be a member of an investigation team. Like Joan, she had faced the original male prejudice until competence and hard work had worn it away. Now nobody could honestly dispute that either Alice or Joan was worthy of her rank.

'Where is it?' the blonde inquired.

'Around the back,' Alice replied. 'In the garage.'

'Do we have anything yet?' Cuchilo asked, glancing to where Brad was still speaking to the two women.

'The victim is Emily Cochran,' the redhead answered. 'She worked in a bookstore in Business. Didn't show for work this morning, so her employer tried to reach her on the

* Why Alice's hair had to be cut short is told in *Run for the Border*.

telephone. The owner of the house, it's her uncle, went to her room and knocked. When he didn't get an answer, he headed for the garage to see if her car was still there. It was. With her lying by it, her skull smashed open.'

'Then?' Joan prompted, making a wry face.

'He called the Lasher house, they sent cars round here and notified Cen-Con. Brad and I were on hand and caught the call. Aren't we the lucky ones?'

'Sure. *You* get your calls at the *beginning* of the watch,' Joan replied. 'What's been done?'

'The photographer's just about finished, the m.e.'s waiting and Brad's with the local fuzz, asking around to see if there were any witnesses.'

'I'd say he's found some,' Cuchilo commented as the blond giant escorted the two women in the deputies direction.

'Alice,' Brad said. 'These ladies may be able to help us. Mrs. Ryan and Mrs. Golightly.'

'We saw the murderer,' Mrs. Ryan announced in a dramatic tone, poking six inches of lanky height over her plump companion's five foot two.

'Of course, we didn't know he'd done anything wrong at the time,' Mrs. Golightly hastened to explain. 'But it must have been him. Why he followed her home and all. She'd hardly turned along the driveway there when he drove up, stopped his car by the sidewalk and went after her.'

'You were on the street?' Joan put in.

The witnesses, middle-aged, neatly dressed and of respectable appearance, turned interested eyes towards the blonde.

'Are you reporters?' Mrs. Ryan wanted to know, making an involuntary move as if to ensure that her hair was tidy.

'This is Deputies Hilton and Cuchilo from our Office,' Alice introduced.

'Oh!' ejaculated the lanky woman, showing just a slight touch of disappointment. 'No, we weren't on the street. It was my night for the Mockingbird Grove Ladies Bridge Club party. We had six tables in my parlour. It just happened that Mrs. Golightly and I were both dummy at the time and were standing by the window.' She waved a hand towards the house across the street from Number Forty-Six. 'Emily

Cochran had just turned in when he drove up. He left his car, walked along the path—'

'She'd gone around the back by then,' Mrs. Golightly interrupted, not wishing to be pushed out of the limelight. 'He must have reached her while she was putting her car into the garage.'

'What time would that be, ma'am?' Cuchilo asked.

'About half past nine,' Mrs. Ryan answered, beating her companion to it by a split second. 'That's one of the reasons I noticed her. She doesn't usually come in that early.'

Joan and Cuchilo exchanged glances. If the woman's estimation of the time was correct, the killer could have murdered Emily Cochran and then gone on to find Amy Willer.

CHAPTER FIVE

'DID you notice what kind of a car the man was driving, ladies?' Cuchilo asked, keeping his thoughts to himself.

'Mercy no!' Mrs. Ryan declared, giving the other witness no chance to say a word. 'It wasn't a convertible like Emily's. I think it was a sedan of some kind. Or a hard-top.'

'It was a Ford Mustang!' Mrs. Golightly put in firmly.

'Fastback or standard?' Alice asked.

'Standard,' the plump woman answered, directing a brief but triumphant glance at Mrs. Ryan. 'It was dark coloured, but I couldn't say what shade.'

'I think it was royal blue,' Mrs. Ryan announced. 'Or it might have been mallard green.'

'You can't be sure—' Mrs. Golightly objected.

'How about the man?' Alice interrupted, knowing better than allow the witnesses to start bickering. 'Can you describe him?'

'Not very well,' Mrs. Ryan admitted. 'This section of the street isn't very well lit at night. It's those children at Thirty-Three, with their BB guns. They're always shooting out the street lights. Why don't you—?'

'*I'll* tell the local Division house to look into it, ma'am,' Brad promised soberly. 'Can you give us any idea what he looked like. Height, build, clothes, anything distinctive about his walk, like that.'

'I'd say he was tall, although not as tall as you and not nearly so well built,' Mrs. Golightly decided, after a moment's thought. 'Slim. Wearing a slouch hat—'

'He was bare-headed,' protested Mrs. Ryan. 'And he wasn't so tall. More medium sized and dumpy. Oh yes. He was wearing glasses.'

With her mouth opening to vehemently deny her companion's description, Mrs. Golightly left the words unsaid.

Instead, she nodded her agreement to Mrs. Ryan's last statement.

'So he was. I saw them glinting in the car's interior lights as he opened the door and got out.'

That was just about the only point upon which the two women reached concurrence. Joan's almost sleepless night had lessened her usual level of tolerance towards unhelpful witnesses, so she wisely left it to Alice and Brad to try to gain something that might help forward the investigation. Neither Mrs. Ryan nor Mrs. Golightly would yield in her description of the man who had followed Emily Cochran. In fact, they could not even agree on his ethnic origin. The lanky woman insisted that the man had been a Negro, but her companion was equally insistent that he was white, or at least Mexican.

'Did you see him leave?' Alice inquired patiently.

'Heavens, no!' Mrs. Ryan snorted. 'I'm not the kind of woman who spies on her neighbours. He hadn't come out when we were called back to the tables.'

'That would be five minutes at the most,' Mrs. Golightly went on.

'Less than that,' objected Mrs. Ryan.

'Did Miss Cochran often have men come home with her?' Brad asked.

'Certainly, she was a beautiful girl,' answered Mrs. Ryan. 'But this one followed her. I don't think she knew he was behind. At least, she didn't look back as she turned on to the driveway.'

'Can you be sure of that, ma'am?' Cuchilo said.

'Certainly,' the lanky woman replied. 'She was in her convertible with the top down.'

'You hadn't seen the man, or the car, outside her home before?' Cuchilo continued.

'Not that I can remember,' Mrs. Ryan admitted. 'There were so many men used to come home with her.'

'We didn't realize that anything was wrong,' Mrs. Golightly injected, determined to exculpate herself from any blame for not having notified the police the previous night. 'Why things like that just don't happen in Mockingbird Grove. This isn't the Bad Bit—'

'Nobody blames you ladies,' Brad put in soothingly. 'If you can spare the time, we like you to go to the Department of Public Safety Building and look at some photographs.'

'Right now?' Mrs. Ryan yelped.

'The longer we delay, the greater chance of the killer escaping, ma'am,' Brad pointed out. 'So, if you could possibly manage to—'

'*I* certainly can!' Mrs. Golightly stated, which was all the inducement her companion needed to comply with the request.

'We'll have you taken and brought back, ladies,' Alice promised. 'So, if you want to collect anything from home—'

'That's the best of being big, handsome and a television personality,' Brad informed the other deputies, watching the women hurrying away to collect hats and handbags. 'You can sure get co-operation from the public.'

'I feel sick,' Cuchilo groaned.

'And me,' Joan agreed. 'Anyways, it looks like it's not only the big, handsome television personalities who can strike oil.'

The Lasher detectives were approaching with two women and a man. While the trio remembered having seen the car, they could not be sure of much more than that. The man claimed that the vehicle had been a light coloured Ford Mustang and that it had not been of the model known as the fastback. All agreed that its driver wore glasses, but could not extend their descriptions beyond that point. They did decide that the time had been around nine-thirty and the man declared that the car had been parked for approximately five minutes. He continued by complaining that the lack of street lighting had prevented him from seeing the driver on the way to the garage or returning; and why didn't the law do something about those damned kids at Number Thirty-Three?

'That gusher sure dried out fast,' Brad drawled, as the witnesses departed with Alice's assurance that the Lasher Division officers would attend to the matter of the kids at Number Thirty-Three.

'At least the feller knew how long the suspect was away

from his car,' Cuchilo reminded the big blond. 'That's more than the Brad Counter fan club could tell us.'

'Jealousy's a terrible thing, isn't it, Brad?' Alice remarked.

'What did I tell you about her, Sam?' Joan sighed, favouring the redhead with a disdainful glare. 'A week.'

'That long at least,' agreed Cuchilo. 'Come on. Let's go and earn our pay, paleface brother and sisters.'

Going to the rear of the house, the four deputies studied the cameraman's Land Polaroid scene-of-the-crime photographs. Then they went to examine the garage and its grisly contents with their own eyes. The medical examiner, a different man from the one on duty the previous night, declined to make a guess at the time of death. He said that he had seen Amy Willer's body earlier that morning and, in his opinion, the wounds were consistent with those inflicted upon Emily Cochran.

'I'll go with the m.e. on that,' Joan commented as the deputies withdrew to the open air. 'Her handbag's been opened and emptied, too.'

'She wasn't wearing any jewellery,' Alice remarked. 'We'll go and talk to her aunt and uncle, Brad.'

'Yo!' agreed the blond giant. Like Cuchilo, he accepted that his partner had more experience in law enforcement and so allowed her to run the team. 'How about you and Joan?'

'We'll wait in the car and see what you turn up,' Joan decided.

Until there was proved a definite connection between the two killings, or they received orders to the contrary, the Cochran investigation was still Alice's and Brad's responsibility. Knowing this, Joan and Cuchilo were staying in the background and leaving the other team to handle things.

While the body was being removed and the S.I.B. search specialists went about their work, Alice and Brad interviewed the dead girl's aunt and uncle. The couple were distressed and shocked by their niece's death, but Mr. Cochran said that he could answer questions. He told them how Emily had gone out on a date. As he and his wife had been away all evening visiting friends, they had not noticed her absence until her employer had telephoned to ask if she would be going into work.

'I don't drive,' Cochran went on. 'So I'd no reason to go to the garage last night. Emily was free to come and go as she pleased, we didn't check up on her. So I—'

'We understand, Mr. Cochran,' Alice told him gently. 'Do you know who Emily was going with on the date?'

'She didn't say, except that it was to see that movie at the Bijou Grande.'

'Was she wearing any jewellery?'

'Sure. A bracelet, rings, wristwatch.'

'Were they valuable?' Alice asked.

'They didn't come from a five and dime,' the man answered. 'But they weren't valuable enough for anybody to kill her for them.'

'How about money?' Brad wanted to know.

'She had some, but I couldn't say how much. Fifty to a hundred dollars, maybe. Not much more.'

'Do you know the names and addresses of any of her friends?' Alice said.

'Men or women?' Cochran queried.

'Both, or either,' Alice told him. 'Perhaps you could give my partner a list, sir. And, if you could, Mrs. Cochran, I'd like you to come with me while I look at your niece's room.'

When Alice and Brad left the house, they had several names and, in some cases, addresses which would need to be checked out. Alice's examination of the dead girl's room had yielded nothing of use. There were letters from her parents in Arizona, but no other correspondence. Her cheque book had no recent entries in it. Although her aunt had looked into the jewel box, she had been unable to say exactly which pieces were missing.

Joan and Cuchilo came towards the other deputies.

'Anything hot?' the blonde asked.

'Not enough to raise a sweat over,' Alice admitted. 'Have the scientifical wonders solved it for us?'

'They say we should look for a feller who talks with a Southern drawl,' Cuchilo grunted. 'And they can't give us any more than that. No finger- or foot-prints. No buttons or threads torn from his jacket. Not even a piece of flowering dogwood blossom of a kind that's only found on the right hand bank of Rockabye Creek half a mile below the lake.'

'I thought Indians were supposed to be strong, silent fellers, Brad,' Alice remarked. 'Let's go—'

'The sheriff called and said for us all to report to his office,' Joan interrupted. 'Unless you pair'd found something hot, that is.'

'Which they haven't,' Cuchilo went on.

'We'll go as soon as I've asked the local fuzz to check on some names,' Alice suggested and grinned at Brad. 'I'll bet the sheriff wants us so that he can ask for your autograph.'

'A week, you said, Joan,' Cuchilo growled, throwing a resigned look at his partner. 'I'll bet it's closer to a month.'

After arranging with the local detectives to visit the names they had been given and who lived in Lasher, Alice and Brad boarded their car. They followed the other team through town to the D.P.S. Building. Ten minutes later, they were seated around the desk in Jack Tragg's office.

The sheriff of Rockabye County was a tall, lean man with short-cropped black hair. Even when wearing his khaki uniform, he conveyed the impression of being clad in a Stetson, calf-skin vest, Levi's pants and high heeled boots with Kelly spurs attached.

Leaning against the wall, the Day Watch Commander, First Deputy McCall, scowled at what he regarded as the pampering of the quartet. Big, gaunt, craggy of features, as dour and weather-beaten as a Scottish Highland's shepherd, he made a contrast to the medium sized, graceful, Latin matinee-idol appearance of his opposite number on the Night Watch. McCall only rarely allowed visitors to his office the use of a chair. In that way, he discouraged them from lingering and wasting his time. However, they were in the sheriff's private sanctum and, although he showed his disapproval, he could not openly object to the four deputies being offered seats.

'What have you so far, Joan?' the sheriff inquired, grinning a little at the glowering First Deputy. He had long since seen through McCall's dour pose, although he – like the rest of the room's occupants – had never seen the Scot without a hat.

'It's not Pinto Soyran we want,' the blonde replied, holding out a sheet of paper she had collected from her desk. 'I.C.R. say he's doing a two-stretch in the Clemens Unit.'*

'Now that's what I'd call a reasonable alibi,' Jack Tragg admitted, taking and studying the paper. 'I see they've given us eight possibles. Ask around and see if any of them are here.'

'Yo!' Joan answered. 'None of their last known locations have turned in reports on them yet.'

In addition to sending the names of criminals with m.o.'s similar to that of Amy Willer's killer, I.C.R. had listed each man's last known address and also requested the law enforcement agencies of the respective towns to inform the Sheriff's Office in Gusher City if the men in question were no longer present. I.C.R. had given another piece of information and Joan was about to comment on it when McCall crossed to the desk.

'There was a series of 1163's† in Houston about three months back,' the First Deputy remarked, showing that he too had read the report. 'The m.o. was near enough the same. This *hombre* used to tag along behind a woman until she stopped her car. Then he'd walk up, pistol whip and rob her. He killed a man and woman on his last caper. The Houston law never caught him, but he quit operating there after that.'

'Could be we've got him,' Brad remarked quietly.

'I hope to hell we haven't,' McCall said fervently. 'He made twelve hits before the last one and left each victim with a bust head.'

'Is there any description of him?' Alice inquired.

'Not enough to yell whoopee over,' McCall replied 'None of his victims could give one and nobody else saw him close enough to help. Just about the only thing they could say was that he wore glasses. And they couldn't all be sure about that.'

'The feller who followed Emily Cochran to the garage

* Clemens Unit: State prison farm at Brazoria, Texas.

† 1163: Texas Penal Code (Offenses Against The Person Section) Article 1163, Assault With Intent To Rob. Penalty, two to ten years' imprisonment.

wore glasses,' Joan commented, 'And, before anybody can tell me, so do a few million other men in these-here United States.'

'Are the two killings tied together?' the sheriff asked.

'I'd say so,' Joan guesssed, after a moment's thought. 'The m.o.'s the same. Everything points to robbery being the motive.'

'We've not come across any connection between the victims,' Brad went on. 'Willer was a loner, according to Joan. Cochran was younger and had more than her share of boy friends. She wasn't on the gambling kick, either. I asked her uncle about it and he reckons she wouldn't even chance a dime in a one-armed bandit at a carnival.'

'We dropped by the Willer place on our way in,' Cuchilo concluded. 'Amy's folks said they'd never heard her mention Emily Cochran and that she bought all her gambling books through the mail, or from a store in Lasher.'

'So all we've got to go on is that he drives a car and wears glasses,' Joan said. 'Which isn't what I'd call a whole heap of help to us.'

'*My* watch doesn't need any more than that,' McCall declared and pretended not to hear Alice's *sotto voce* comment of, 'You want to bet?'

'Can I leave Alice and Brad on it, Mac?' asked the sheriff.

'Aye,' confirmed McCall. 'I was looking for some work to give them.'

'You'll be on it, then,' Jack told the redhead and the blond giant. 'Do you need any more help, Joan?'

Flickering a glance at Brad, Alice gave a quick smile. In a tactful manner, the sheriff had let it be known who would be commanding the investigation. One of the things which made Jack Tragg such an efficient law enforcement administrator was that he never overlooked the small personal details when dealing with a major crime.

'We'll be enough,' the blonde decided. 'R. and I. came up with five possibles. We'll split them between us. You check out the bookstore for a connection between Willer and Cochran, Alice. Sam and I'll talk to the folks at Euro-Tex.'

'Yo!' Alice replied. 'There'll be Cochran's friends to check out while we're at it.'

'Yeah,' Joan drawled. 'I'm starting to wish I'd asked for more help.'

'You Night Watch crowd want things too easy,' McCall growled. 'By the way, Fred saw his nephew and that other yack. Bawled the hell out of them and told them to get the hell out of Rockabye County. We turned them and their girls loose and passed Fred to the blue-noses. You can forget that side of it.'

One of the three telephones on the desk beeped. Picking up the receiver, Jack Tragg listened, then said, 'Put them through.' Covering the mouthpiece with his left hand, he looked at the deputies. 'It's the Hollywood Police Department.'

By the time the call had ended, Joan held a list of four names and addresses in Gusher City and two more within the boundaries of the county.

'One in Lasher, just outside Mockingbird Grove,' the blonde said. 'We'll try him first. One in Evans Hill, Leander and Jepson. We'll have the Sub-Offices take the out-of-town addresses, if that's all right with you, sir.'

'It'll save time,' the sheriff confirmed. 'All right, if there's nothing more, we'll break this up. If you need anything else, Joan, ask for it.'

'We'll do just that,' Joan promised and came to her feet. 'Something tells me this is going to be a long day.'

None of the blonde's companions gave her an argument on that point. While the four deputies believed that the killings had been the work of one man in the commission of robberies, they knew better than to overlook the possibility of coincidence or that there might be some other motive. So they faced a long session of locating, visiting and interviewing people. They also knew that much of the time they would be running into dead ends.

'I'll have Houston send us a full report on those 1163's,' Joan remarked as the two teams gathered around her desk for a council of war before setting out on their investigations. 'It may give us a lead.'

'Sure,' Alice agreed. 'Jack's asked Hollywood to send us and I.C.R. a list of all Glam-Batt's customers in Texas. That might get us a few more names.'

'Should we ask the blue-noses to prowl their bookstores and see if any local hoods go for the girl fight bit?' Brad inquired.

'Like Mac'd say, it'll give them something to do for their pay,' Cuchilo grinned, then became serious. 'Hell. We don't even know that that piece of the brochure's anything to do with the case.'

At that moment, in an office not half a mile from the D.P.S. Building, a man was picking up a telephone.

'Oscar,' said a voice he recognized as his wife's. 'Are you alone?'

'Of course,' he replied.

'I've just been looking at the latest Glam-Batt brochure—' the wife began.

'Oh that,' he interrupted. 'I tore it up and put it in my brown suit's pocket. I was going to throw it in the waste-paper bin, but you know what a nosy old bitch Mrs. Raymet is. She might have put the pieces together while she was cleaning the room—'

'*I* put them together,' the wife cut in. 'There's a piece missing. It's not in the house, or the garage.'

'Perhaps it's in the car—'

'Or in the one you used last night!'

'It could be. But I shouldn't worry too much, dear. There's no way the brochure can be traceed to us, even if the piece is found. It was forwarded from Houston, don't forget. Are you ready for tonight?'

'You can bet your sweet bippy I am,' the woman declared enthusiastically. 'In fact, if she's all you say, I can hardly wait.'

CHAPTER SIX

WHAT Broadway means to New York, or the Piccadilly Circus-Leicester Square area is to London, The Street was to Gusher City. There could be found the major movie or live theatres, the best night clubs and cafes. If a visitor wanted other forms of entertainment, most needs could be satisfied in the alleys and streets which connected to The Street. A man in search of female company need only select his turning from The Street and he would find girls like Mabel Liebeck willing to supply it.

Not, Mabel thought as she stepped out of the Bucket Of Blood Bar and looked along the alley towards The Street, that anybody was being trampled to death in the crush to be kept company. A tall, good looking woman, black haired and possessing a rich, full-breasted, slim-waisted, wide-hipped figure that a white mini-dress, black tights and high heeled pumps showed to its best advantage, Mabel was a prostitute. She felt no shame in her profession, knowing that she was good at it and still able to hold her own against competition from younger hookers. Only there was no need for competition. Tuesday in the middle of the month had always been a poor day for girls in her line of business.

A man turned hesitantly into the alley, pausing in its mouth as if debating whether to advance or go back to The Street. Mabel studied him with shrewd eyes, deciding that he was a business prospect. There was only one thing wrong. Before he reached her, he had to pass Marty's Grill; and that was the regular hang-out of her main competitor. Della Zekov would not pass up such a likely mark if he went in, especially if she saw the chance of doing it in front of Mabel.

With that thought in mind, Mabel started to slink sensually towards the man. By an unwritten agreement, the hookers who used the alley kept to their own bars; but a man on the street was fair game. Della might not like seeing Mabel near Marty's Grill, but would not make trouble about it right then.

Advancing a few steps into the alley, the man was looking at Mabel with considerable interest. She returned his scrutiny with a gaze that calculated his value as a customer. The well-cut, sober brown suit, white shirt, quiet bow tie and shoes had come from expensive shops and he sported a wrist-watch that must have set him back plenty. Yes, he was a good prospect. Not, however, that he was an imposing physical specimen. Five foot five at the most and slender with it, he had a meek cast of features which were not strengthened by a pair of round, gold rimmed glasses or a pencil thin moustache.

Mabel did not allow his mousey, insignificant appearance to put her off. Early in her career, she had become reconciled to the idea that big, handsome fellers with the Mr. Universe bodies did not need to come looking, or paying, for girls to roll in the hay with them.

'Hi there, handsome,' Mabel greeted, gliding closer and taking a cigarette from her handbag. 'Do you have a light?'

'Er – Yes!' the man replied, acting in a startled, fluttery and nervous manner which the hooker found most amusing.

Taking out a silver cigarette lighter, the man flicked it into life. As he held it forward, Mabel's hands cupped around his and squeezed them in gentle invitation. While lighting the cigarette, she looked at him and fought to keep her mixture of contempt and amusement from showing. Going by his anxious behaviour, he had never been involved in such a situation. With the cigarette glowing, she removed her hands and smiled at him.

'Are you looking for somebody?'

'Er – No – Well, yes, I am.'

'Would it be anybody I'm likely to know?' Mabel inquired.

'Humph!' coughed the man, eyes roaming up and down devouring her openly displayed charms. 'Well – er – I'm not exactly looking for anybody. This is my first visit to Gusher City. I only arrived this morning.'

'You'll not know many folks here then,' Mabel remarked casually, but wanting to get to the point. They were standing outside Marty's Grill and Della might regard that as poaching on her territory. 'Or are you here with your wife?'

While speaking, Mabel was conscious of the man's eyes on her face. He had stopped ogling her curves and was staring up with an almost wary alertness. As if becoming aware that she had noticed the direction of his gaze, he looked down at her bosom.

'Er – No. I'm alone. I – Er – That is – Would you think it presumptuous of me if I was to offer to buy you a drink?'

'That's it, you short-grown bastard,' Mabel thought. 'Get to the point.' Audibly, she said, 'Why not? The Bucket Of Blood along there's a reg—'

'Well – Humph! – It's – I – Er – I wondered if we might have it somewhere a little more – private – If that's all right with you?'

'We could always go up to my place,' Mabel suggested, still trying to conceal the amusement she felt at his perturbation.

'Well – Humph! You – er – mistake—!' the man spluttered.

'How's that?' Mabel demanded.

'Er – You may think this is a little strange, but, well – that is—'

'What's with you, honey?'

'You see,' the man replied and appeared to be steeling himself for an effort of some kind. When he went on, the words came out with a rush. 'You see, I work for Mr. – an executive on the board of Trans-Atlantic Oil. I'm his p.a.—'

'Should pay well,' Mabel remarked, showing greater interest.

'It's quite remunerative. But I have to carry out some unusual tasks outside my normal duties. Like right now, for instance.'

'What's with right now?'

'Well – er – H.B. – my employer – He has sent me to find a

charming young lady who is willing to spend the night with him.'

'Huh?' grunted the hooker, hiding her elation and trying to simulate the kind of surprised reaction she felt would be expected.

'He said for me to come to The Street and pick the best looking young lady I could find,' the man went on. 'If she's agreeable, I'm to offer her five hundred dollars to come and spend the night with him.'

'F – Five hundred—?' Mabel gulped.

'If you don't feel that it is enough,' the man said stiffly, darting a look at Marty's Grill, 'I'll try to find somebody else.'

'Slow down, honey, I'll come. Say, why don't I get a friend for you?'

'I'm afraid I must decline. Once I've taken you to H.B., I have other matters to which I must attend. By the way. There is one condition to this. You must come in my vehicle and not know where I take you.'

'Well now—', Mabel began hesitantly.

'You must understand H.B. – my employer's position,' the man told her. 'Nobody knows he is in Gusher City. If word was to leak out, it would queer our de – It would be most inconvenient. I'm afraid you must come on my terms, or not at all.'

Having delivered his ultimatum, the small man made as if to turn towards the Grill. Mabel thought fast. She had found herself faced with the fulfilment of every hooker's dream, an invitation to entertain an important business executive. A girl never knew where such a proposition might end. Certainly it was an opportunity which she would be a fool to pass up. If nothing else emerged from the assignation, she would be five hundred dollars better off. And there must be a market in the city for information concerning the mysterious H.B.'s presence.

'I'll do it!' Mabel said. 'Just let me go tell the bartender at the Bucket Of Blood that I'm—'

'I'm afraid not,' the man answered. 'You must understand the need for secrecy. I can't take chances. If you feel that you might not receive your payment, or not be permitted to keep it, let me offer a suggestion. I have a stamped envelope in my pocket. You can put your – fee – in it and mail it to your home. Unless, of course, you don't feel it would be safe with your room-mates.'

'I live alone,' Mabel replied. 'That's a smart notion you've got.'

'I've handled this kind of thing before,' the man assured her. 'Shall we go? I noticed a mailbox near where I parked my car and we won't attract any attention there.'

Accompanying the man from the alley, Mabel did not worry about her failure to notify Larry at the bar of her departure. She was not some first-night kid who needed to be watched to make sure that she did not try to cheat on the Syndicate. Having been in the business for more years than she cared to remember, she knew that her employers trusted her to turn in her quota. So if Larry did not see her around, he would realize that she had picked up and gone off with a mark. She had done it often enough for it to be no cause of alarm.

Nor did the hooker feel any concern over the unusual aspects of her assignation. Maybe she would not have been so eager to accept if trade had been better; but one did not look a gift horse with five hundred dollar teeth in the mouth on a slack Tuesday night. As long as the little guy kept up his end of the bargain, she could go along secure in the knowledge that her money was safe. If he tried to welsh, she would not even need to get into his car.

On being escorted into the parking lot of the Bijou Grande movie theatre, Mabel felt surprised, and a little suspicious, at the sight of the vehicle to which the man was leading her It was a raven black Jeepster Commando station wagon with its rear section converted into a windowless compartment. Either the man had been lucky, or he had selected his parking position with care. The mail box was directly in front of the vehicle, beyond the lot's low wall.

'We came in by road to avoid attracting attention,' the man remarked, explaining away the source of Mabel's suspicions. 'As I told you, H.B. – I've had to do this kind of thing before.'

'I can see that,' the hooker admitted.

Taking out his wallet, the man counted five one hundred dollar bills from its interior. After handing over the money, he produced an envelope and a ball-point pen. With her fee inside, Mabel sealed down the flap and, resting the envelope on the hood, wrote her home address on it. Straightening up, she found that the man had moved closer and was peering at the envelope. Becoming aware that she had observed his interest, he jerked his gaze away.

'How about mailing this for me?' the girl inquired. 'If I try climbing over that wall, I'll show everything I've got.'

'That would never do,' the man replied soberly.

Taking the envelope, Mabel's escort stepped over the wall. A grin twisted at her lips as she watched him. Going by the way he had acted, he wanted to learn her name and address. Maybe he fancied a roll in the hay at some later date and Mabel believed in encouraging potential customers.

Making no attempt to put the envelope out of the girl's sight, the man dropped it into the mailbox. Returning, he unlocked the rear door of the Jeepster, clicked on an interior light and motioned for Mabel to enter. Climbing in, she found it to be equipped with comfortable seats. Not until the door was closed did she notice that it had no handle on the inside and was the only way of entering or leaving the compartment. Although the walls had ventilation slits, she could not see through them. Whoever that important exec. might be, he sure was not intending to take chances of her discovering where he was staying.

After a brief pause, during which Mabel suspected that the little man was making a note of her name and address, the Jeepster started moving. Completely enclosed, the girl could form no notion of the direction they took, nor at what speed they might be travelling. At last, the vehicle swerved sharply to the right, bounced a little as if mounting a sidewalk, dipped downwards and came to a halt. She thought that she could hear a garage door opening, then the Jeepster advanced a short distance and halted again. Its engine was cut and she heard footsteps approaching the rear of the compartment.

On opening the rear door, the man allowed Mabel to

reach it. Then, taking her by the hand, he turned out the interior light. Helping her jump down he gripped her arm and guided her through the darkness of what she guessed to be an underground garage. She thought that she could see the dark bulk of another vehicle, but could form no impression as to its make or type. The opportunity to do so was denied her.

A sudden flood of bright light dazzled Mabel as the man jerked open a door. By the time she could see clearly again, he had led her forward and closed the door behind them. Peering around, she found that she was standing in a large basement which appeared to be part gymnasium and part photographer's studio. Across the room from where she stood was a thick, tarpaulin covered wrestling mat. On a table close to the mat lay a pair of boxing gloves, a couple of towels and bottles of smelling salts or other medicaments. Powerful lights illuminated the mat. A movie – and two still-cameras on tripods were positioned around it. In a corner, a plastic bucket stood under a water faucet in a sink.

'I'm afraid I've been misleading you somewhat, Miss Liebeck,' the man remarked, making no attempt to cross the basement to its second door.

'How do you mean?' the girl inquired.

'There isn't any rich oil executive here. The whole story was a little white lie to persuade you to accompany me on my terms.'

If the man had been bigger, or in any way more impressive-looking, Mabel might have felt scared. That mousey little *hombre* did not frighten her. Why, if he tried anything, she could chew him up and spit out the hard bits. Instead of being concerned by his statement, Mabel felt sure that she could guess at why he had lied to her. Probably he had never laid a girl before. He looked like the kind of milksop who had lived all his life under the thumb of a domineering mother and was grabbing an opportunity to roll in the hay. Most likely his mother was away from home and he was trying to show his manly independence by fetching the girl there. That could account for the elaborate precautions.

Well, for five hundred dollars, Mabel figured that she

could put up with being told a 'little white lie'. In return for her fee, she would give him a night he would remember for the rest of his life.

'It's *you* who wants me, huh?' she asked.

'Well,' the man admitted, looking even more meek and inoffensive. 'I won't deny it. I do want you.'

'How about your wife?'

'I'm – er – not married. My mother – Well, she's on vacation and we have the house to ourselves.'

'I hate crowds. Aren't you the foxy one, though. Let's go out of—'

'There's just one thing,' the man said, almost apologetically. 'As you see, my hobby is photography. So I wondered if I could – That is – Er – Would you let me take some pictures of you?'

'Sure,' Mabel grinned, seeing the way opening to make more money. 'Where do you want me to stand?'

'Well, I – Er – Humph! I mean undressed.'

'Well now,' Mabel began with false hesitancy. 'I don't usually—'

'I – I won't be ungrateful,' the man assured her, dipping his left hand into his jacket pocket and producing a charm bracelet. 'Perhaps this will—'

'It will,' Mabel agreed, testing the weight of the offering and deciding that it was gold. One of the charms had been broken off, but the bracelet would still bring around fifty dollars if she wanted to sell it. 'Shall I peel off?'

'Please do,' affirmed the man. 'Put the bracelet in your handbag and do so by all means.'

'Do you want me raw?' the girl inquired, complying with the suggestion and crossing to place her bag on the table.

'Good heavens, no. Keep your tights on.'

'And shoes?'

'I think not. Your – er – legs don't need any embellishments.'

'Anyway you want it, Mr. – ? Say, do we have to be so formal?'

'Call me "Mark",' the man suggested.

Reaching behind her, Mabel unzipped the dress and

wriggled out of it. She could imagine the use Mark would have for his photographs. In a few days, he would most likely be showing them around the office and boasting that she was a girl he had met and laid on his last vacation. If he was unlucky in who he showed them to, he could easily be exposed as a liar by one of her other customers.

'Is this your gym?' she asked, placing the dress on the table.

'It's mine,' Mark agreed, studying her with much less emotion than she would have expected. There was interest and anticipation in his gaze, but little of the embarrassment that she had thought he would display.

With the weather being so warm, Mabel had been wearing the minimum of clothes. Her figure was good enough to do away with the need for artificial aids. So she turned, allowing him to feast his gaze on her body. Clad only in a bra and the tights, she reckoned he would be breaking out in a sweat at the sight. Why not give him another thrill?

'How about unfastening my bra, Mark?'

'Of course,' the man answered and did so.

Peeling the bra from her jutting bosom, Mabel grinned. She had felt his hands trembling as he fumbled with the fastenings and had been conscious of his breath coming quicker. Yet he withdrew without even touching her up. Having the photographs taken would help to pass some of what looked like being a very dull evening.

If the girl had turned as soon as the bra was free, she might have noticed the man throw a glance and nod towards the second of the basement's doors. It was open about an inch, but no light shone through from whatever lay beyond its portals.

Slowly, sensually, thrusting forward her bust to give 'Mark' its full, voluptuous impact, Mabel turned. To her surprise, she found that he had moved away and was taking off his jacket.

'Everything all right?' she demanded, a little annoyed by his apparent lack of interest.

'Certainly,' the man agreed, placing his jacket on the table and removing his bow tie to open his shirt's neck. Despite his indifferent attitude, he was sweating. 'Now for your pose. I see you as an Amazon, a proud female warrior. It's a pity that we don't have a sword and shield for you. Perhaps the boxing gloves will convey the correct impression of martial spirit. Will you put them on, please?'

'Anything you say,' Mabel replied, picking up the left hand glove.

'You'll find it easier if you take off all your jewellery,' the man warned. 'If the rings catch in the lining, you'll hurt yourself taking the gloves off.'

'How about letting me have some when they're developed?' Mabel suggested, taking his advice and dropping her jewellery into her handbag. 'You can fetch them around, I'm mostly at the Bucket of Blood.'

'I'll do that,' the man promised, fastening the tapes of the gloves for her. 'I suppose a girl in your line of business has to know how to defend herself?'

'It helps,' Mabel admitted and, feeling that a word of warning might be in order, continued, 'I'm a tough cookie. Not that I've ever done any boxing, mind.'

'We can't have everything, I suppose,' the man answered. 'Will you go out into the centre of the mat?'

Somehow, Mabel thought as she obeyed, 'Mark' seemed different. The air of hesitant nervousness had left him. With his jacket off, he seemed to have developed a more robust torso than she would have expected. Mabel had never been unduly sensitive to atmosphere, but she felt a trifle uneasy at the change in the small man.

'How's this for a pose?' the girl asked, throwing off her vague sense of perturbation. She adopted the type of stancc favoured by old-time bare-knuckle pugilists.

'It's not what I want,' the man replied in firmer, more decisive tones than he had used previously. 'There's one thing more we need to make a perfect picture.'

'What would that be?' Mabel demanded suspiciously.

Suddenly the girl felt a sense of deep foreboding. Something in the man's attitude hinted that the situation was far less harmless than she had previously imagined. 'Mark' stood alongside the movie camera, which was not the device she would have expected him to use, and eyed her with mocking, yet lascivious delight.

'Why an opponent for you, of course,' the man said and raised his voice. 'We're ready for you, Hippolyta my dear.'

CHAPTER SEVEN

HEARING the sound of a door opening, Mabel swung around to find out who had entered. A low gasp of amazement burst from her at the sight which met her startled eyes.

Standing by his camera, Oscar Burgenhof felt a surge of delight as he studied Mabel's reactions. From the first moment in the alley, the hooker had regarded him with an infuriating mixture of amusement and contempt. Taking in his appearance, she had discounted him as a real man. All the time he had been playing his part in the deception, he had been boiling with rage internally. Only the knowledge of what lay ahead had enabled him to keep in the character of the hesitant milksop.

Ever since he was a child, members of the opposite sex had treated him in the same manner and he hated them for it.

All women except Hippolyta, that is.

From their first meeting, she had always shown him respect, devotion and love. More than that, she had been willing to help him take revenge on her own sex for having spurned, mocked or disregarded him on account of his small size and insignificant appearance. Of course, Hippolyta and he shared a common interest which bound them closer together

Kicking the door closed behind her, Mrs. Burgenhof advanced towards the well-lit mat. But it was not a Mrs. Burgenhof any of the neighbours or her acquaintances would have recognized. Gone was the unalluring mousey-brown wig and shape-ruining, figure-concealing clothes in which she usually presented herself to the outside world. Short-cropped, curly tawny hair framed a face that glowed in excited, almost ecstatic anticipation far different from her everyday expression of placid, near-vacant disinterest.

Nobody would call Mrs. Burgenhof beautiful, her features were plain although not repulsive. However, wearing nothing but brief white satin panties and a pair of boxing gloves, she proved to have a body every bit as well-developed as that of the prostitute. There was a savage, cat-like grace to the woman's movements, made even more so by the play of her firm, hard, calf, thigh, body and arm muscles. Not only was she a magnificently built woman, but she was also a remarkably fit and powerful one.

Once on the mat, Hippolyta Burgenhof adopted the stance of a modern boxer. With her weight balanced lightly on the balls of feet spread a shoulder's width apart, she put up her fists. Her left elbow was bent and behind the left glove. The right elbow was tucked vertically below its glove which protected her drawn in chin. Everything about her told of trained readiness.

Staring from Burgenhof to his wife and back, Mabel felt the growing realization that she had made a terrible mistake. What had started off by seeming like a golden opportunity was rapidly turning into a situation of bizarre horror. The tawny haired woman was dancing, bobbing and shadow boxing in the way Mabel had seen a fighter act before the start of a bout. Crouching behind the movie camera, her husband was making adjustments to its lens.

'Who – What—?' Mabel spluttered, unable to put her thoughts into more coherent speech.

'You did say I could take some pictures of you,' Burgenhof pointed out, revelling in the hooker's growing signs of concern. 'So that's what I intend to do. Take *moving* pictures of two Amazons embroiled in conflict. Start when you're ready, my love.'

'Hey! Just a blasted minute!' Mabel yelped, the words coming out with a rush as the man moved into position to operate the camera. Getting no response from him, she turned to face the woman. 'I didn't figure on anything—'

Bouncing closer, Hippolyta stabbed forward her left hand. The padded leather of the glove's knuckle jabbed against Mabel's face hard enough to snap her head back, and chopped off her protest. Retreating with tears bursting from her eyes, the girl felt a hot trickle of blood dribbling from her nostrils. The pain brought an instant reaction from her. Squealing in fury, she flung herself wildly at her attacker. Mabel's fists met only air. Weaving clear, Hippolyta shot out her left again. Raw agony blazed through the girl as the glove impacted on her left breast. Hands flying to the point of impact, Mabel again moved backwards.

With her face glowing in savage exultation, the tawny-haired woman danced after her victim. Crouching behind the camera, Burgenhof kept its mechanism turning. His features matched his wife's expression.

A right hook to the stomach robbed Mabel of the breath she had been preparing to expend in a scream for help. Doubling over, she saw brown leather, spattered with her blood, rushing up at her. The glove took her full in the centre of the face. Lifted erect, she tumbled on to her back. Sobbing and clasping her hands to her face, she managed to roll onto her stomach.

'Get up!' Hippolyta ordered, hooking her right foot under the girl's left shoulder and turning her over.

'Come on now, Mabel', Burgenhof went on, stopping and leaving the camera to advance and stand at his wife's side. 'This is hardly giving us value for our five hundred dollars. It isn't to be had as easily as all that.'

'Y–Y–You ba – bas – bastards!' Mabel sobbed, trying to shuffle away from the couple.

'Get this, you two-bit hooker!' Hippolyta spat, placing her left foot on the girl's belly and pinning her to the mat. 'The only girl fight movies we can buy are fakes, obvious fakes at that. So we're going to make our own movie and we've brought you here to help do it.'

'G – Go to hell!' Mabel croaked, squirming in an attempt to escape from the pressure of the woman's foot.

'If you don't get up and fight, you're going to wish you had,' Burgenhof warned and there was nothing left of the hesitant little milksop in his attitude. 'You see, if we can't get a fight on film, we'll have to make do with footage of bondage and torture. Whipping with a quirt to be precise. You wouldn't like that at all.'

'Some of those bondage ties can cripple you for life, or kill you,' Hippolyta elaborated. 'You know what we're talking about?'

Thoroughly terrified, Mabel nodded. The bartender at the Bucket of Blood kept a stock of bondage photographs and similar items for sale to customers. Although she could not think why anybody would want to buy such things, Mabel had seen enough of them to remember the bizarre and uncomfortable ways in which the models had been tied up.

'There are ties which are so dangerous they daren't do them on a live model and only illustrate in cartoon folders,' Burgenhof continued, '*We* don't suffer from any such scruples.'

Having delivered their warnings, the Burgenhofs bent and lifted Mabel to her feet. Fear showed plainly on her face and she stared around, desperately seeking for a means of escape.

'There's no way out,' the woman informed her. 'Both doors are locked. This part of the basement is completely sound proof. You could scream your head off and nobody outside will hear you.'

'So save your breath and use it to put up a good fight,' Burgenhof advised.

Sucking in deep, gasping breaths of air, Mabel turned her frightened gaze from the man to his wife and back. She tried to tell herself that it was all a hideous nightmare from which she would awaken shortly. Yet the throbbing ache in her bust, the taste of the blood from her nose as it ran over her lips and feel of the mat under her feet warned that it really was happening.

'All right, get ready,' Burgenhof said, having returned to the camera. He crouched behind it, took aim and reached for the starter button. 'Give me some action on "three". One. Two. Three.'

'Come on, hooker!' Hippolyta mocked, when Mabel made no movement. Placing her hands on her hips, the woman stood squarely facing the girl and went on, 'This is your chance. Come and try to hit me.'

'Hit you!' Mabel screamed, fury overriding fear. 'I'll kill you!'

With that, the girl lunged and swung a round-house right calculated to strike Hippolyta's face and stretch her out cold. After which, Mabel intended to teach her runt of a husband a lesson he would never forget. By the time she got through with them, the couple would be allergic to girl fight movies for the rest of their lives.

Moving with almost contemptuous ease, Hippolyta interposed her own right glove between Mabel's fist and her face. Although her punch was halted before reaching its target, the girl's impetus caused her to continue to advance. Like a flash, Hippolyta dug a sharp left hook just above the black tights. Gasping and clutching at the area, Mabel threw herself to the rear a couple of strides. For all that, she remained on her feet. Anger caused her to be determined to avenge the pain she had suffered at the woman's hands. Glaring ahead, she saw Hippolyta approaching. Not in the well-guarded posture this time, but with the gloves dangling by her sides and torso exposed.

Fighting down the pain and nausea which beat at her, the girl straightened her wobbly legs and thrust forward her left glove. With a sickening – yet to Mabel, satisfying – thud, the blow smashed full into Hippolyta's bobbing left breast. Shock and agony twisted at the woman's face and an involuntary cry of anguish burst from her lips. Having suffered a similar blow, Mabel expected to see Hippolyta collapse. Although she reeled and her features contorted with the suffering, the woman did not go down.

Determined to make the most of her advantage, the girl ran at Hippolyta and swung her arms like flails. Time after time the gloves whacked against the woman's head and body, keeping her staggering on the verge of losing her balance. Only Mabel's inexperience saved Hippolyta from suffering serious damage. The girl did not know how to throw a punch correctly. She started the woman's nose bleeding, but failed to connect with a punch which would incapacitate Hippolyta.

Believing that she was inflicting more damage than was the case, Mabel expected 'Mark' to intervene and save his wife from further punishment. Taking her attention from Hippolyta, she looked around. To her amazement, she found that the man was still hunched over the camera and keeping it operating.

That look proved to be a bad mistake!

Given even such a small respite, Hippolyta had recovered her equilibrium. Mabel became aware of the changed situation when she felt the other's gloves thudding into her torso. Forgetting 'Mark's' behaviour, the girl started to hit back at her assailant.

Standing toe to toe in the centre of the mat, while a freely perspiring Burgenhof recorded the scene on film, the two magnificently developed women traded punches. There was a difference in the way they attacked each other. Where Mable swung wildly and without skill, Hippolyta aimed her gloves with trained and deliberate purpose. The girl left herself wide open all the time, presenting a woman of Hippolyta's ability with numerous opportunities to land a knockout blow. Wanting to keep the fight going for as long as possible, the woman refrained from taking advantage of the girl's inexperience.

For almost two minutes without a pause, the exchange of blows continued. The two women, naked busts jiggling and bouncing in time to their movements or on receiving punches, beat remorselessly at each other. They barely moved a foot in either direction from the centre of the mat. By accident, or design on Hippolyta's part, they were standing sideways on to the camera so that it could gather in almost every detail of the action on its turning reel of film. Blood flowed freely from their nostrils and Mabel's lips, sweat coated them in glistening sheens, but their arms never ceased to move.

Suddenly Mabel made a discovery which scared her even more than the precarious nature of her situation, or the possibility of disfigurement to her face. Withdrawing slightly, by instinct rather than intention, the girl threw and landed a heavy punch on Hippolyta's right breast. Instead of showing agony, or displaying a desire to avoid further punishment, the woman's sweating, bloody face twisted into an expression of raw, primeval ecstasy. Instead of attempting to shield her bust, Hippolyta almost appeared to be offering it as a target for further attacks.

Panic, far worse than any she had experienced since entering the basement, tore at Mabel. She was now aware that the woman was enjoying receiving the pain as much as handing it out.

That knowledge proved to be the final straw for Mabel. With each blow given and received in return, she had felt her will to resist decreasing. Only a mixture of courage, anger and desperation had kept her going for so long. Although she exercised sufficiently to retain her body's man-attracting curves – she had learned the lesson early from the fate of other hookers who had failed to take that precaution – her way of life was not conducive to complete physical fitness. With the realization, the rage-induced excitement, which had kept Mabel almost impervious to the pain caused by Hippolyta's blows, ebbed away. She became aware of an ever-increasing, gnawing torment raging through her body. Tears and sweat half blinded her. It called for a continuous effort to drag air into her lungs. White-hot agony blazed through her whole being as Hippolyta's left glove hooked wickedly into the base of her bust. Croaking what would have been a scream, if she had had sufficient breath to produce one, Mabel tottered clear of the other woman.

Hissing with delight and triumph, Hippolyta crowded in on the girl. With arms working like piston rods, she beat mercilessly at the helpless Mabel's head and torso. Then, as the hooker's eyes glazed and legs began to buckle under her, Hippolyta brought the torment to an end. Taking a stride to the rear, the woman flung up a long right cross. Hard packed leather collided with solid force against the side of Mabel's jaw. The girl's head was flung back and she crashed limply to the mat.

Sucking in deep, long breaths, Hippolyta stood for a moment glaring down at the supine motionless figure. Then the woman stepped around to confront the camera and placed her right foot on Mabel's bosom. Raising her hands above her head in the boxer's traditional victory salute, Hippolyta stood in that posture for several seconds. Face glowing with a variety of emotions, Burgenhof stopped the camera and stepped around it on to the mat.

'Marvellous, my dear,' the man congratulated, approaching his wife with open arms. 'We got some wonderful footage so far.'

Lowering her hands, Hippolyta stepped over Mabel with no more display of interest than if the girl had been made of wood. Although her bust pitched and heaved from the exertion of the past minutes, she flung herself into her husband's arms. Oblivious of the blood which splashed on to him from her nostrils, Burgenhof kissed her passionately.

'It was wonderful!' Hippolyta hissed on being released from the embrace. Wriggling her body in a frenzy of ecstasy, she went on, 'Let's bring her round, Oscar. I want to fight some more.'

'Very well, my dear,' the man replied eagerly. 'But we've time for each other first.'

Slowly Mabel Liebeck swung her legs from the bed and eased her protesting body into a sitting position. A telephone was ringing somewhere close by, the sound jarring painfully at her throbbing head with wicked persistence. For all that, the aches and pains which had torn at her since the start of the first fight were somewhat diminished. At least, she could now move beyond the horizontal without wanting to throw up her guts.

A low moan broke from her and she tried to stifle it. If that crazy pair of bastards had heard, they would know that she had regained consciousness and start to beat her up again. She wondered why they had brought her into this darkened bedroom. On the other occasions, they had left her where she had fallen and made love while waiting for her to come round. Once she had recovered, they had resumed with their tortures. On recovering from the boxing knockout, she had been washed, had the bleeding stopped and was made ready for the next session. With the boxing gloves replaced by an elbow-length pair of black nylon, she had been made to fight Hippolyta in a hair-yanking brawl. The woman's superior physical condition and strength had brought about Mabel's defeat. On the next return to consciousness, the girl had been placed in a series of wrestling holds while 'Mark' used the still cameras.

A shudder ran through Mabel as she remembered one particular pose. It had given her complete proof that Hippolyta was the kind of nut who delighted in having physical pain inflicted on her. What could a girl do against a wierdo of that kind?

Through the waves of dizziness which filled her, a sense of realization came to Mabel. There was no wonder that she had thought the room looked vaguely familiar. It was her own apartment. Somehow 'Mark' and Hippolyta had transferred her from their basement to her living quarters and left her naked on the bed.

Turning her head as swiftly as her stiff neck muscles would permit, Mabel stared about her. Although she had no idea of what the time might be, daylight showed through the drawn drapes of the window. All her clothes, including her tattered, ruined tights, lay on the bedside chair and were folded far more neatly than she every bothered to do it. Lifting her gaze, she took in the sight of her handbag and jewellery on the dressing table.

Then a startled exclamation burst from her lips.

The face which grimaced at her from the table's mirror was one she barely recognized. Topped by what looked more like a tangled, matted animal's mane than once immaculately coiffured hair, its left eye was swollen completely closed. Equally discoloured, the right was a puffed up, narrow slit. No wonder her nose felt clogged up and twice its normal size – it looked that way. Both lips' normal fullness had almost doubled in size and the top one was split. Continuing her scrutiny, she discovered that her torso, especially the bosom, had an extensive mottling of bruises.

Lord! That tawny haired bastard had really worked her over!

Why the hell didn't that telephone stop ringing?

It showed no inclination of doing so and Mabel knew that she must do something to change things. Painfully she rose and, swaying slightly, hobbled across the room. The telephone stood on a small table to the right of the front door. A blank envelope leaned against the instrument and a second – this time stamped and addressed – lay on the floor beneath the letterbox. Ignoring them in her desire to bring the ringing to a halt, she picked up the receiver and held it to her right ear. Her legs wobbled under the strain and she sank to sit on the table.

'Mabel?' asked a male voice which sounded vaguely familiar.

'Yeah,' she confirmed through her swollen lips, thinking that the last thing she wanted right then was for a regular customer to be calling to arrange for a roll in the hay. 'Who is this?'

' "Mark",' was the reply.

CHAPTER EIGHT

STIFFENING sharply, then wincing at the pain caused by her incautious movement, Mabel stared at the receiver. No doubt about it, that *was* 'Mark's' voice; but subtly different. Harder, grimmer, much more masterful and with none of the apologetic hesitancy which had coloured his speech and behaviour when they had first met in the alley off The Street.

'Mark!' the girl croaked furiously. 'Why you—!'

'Shut up and listen!' the voice cut in, throbbing with such concentrated venom that she could not help but obey. 'My wife and I have decided that by this time you should be recovered sufficiently to understand what I'm saying. If you aren't, tell me and I'll call you later.'

'I can understand, you stin—!' Mabel yelled and wished she had not for the sound made her head ache.

'Then do it!' Burgenhof interrupted. 'You're probably wondering how you can get even with us for last night?'

'You can just bet I am!'

'Take my advice and forget it.'

'Forget—!'

'That's what I said. *You* don't know how to find us. As you can see, *we* know your home address. So, if we need to, *we* can find *you*.'

'I'll have you found—!' Mabel began.

'Don't think that licence plate you may have memorized will be of any help,' Burgenhof warned. 'It's a fake. There's no way the police could trace the vehicle to us.'

'*Police?*' Mabel snorted. 'The folks I'll tell are more wise-up than any damned fuzz.'

'You probably mean the Syndicate, or whatever your organization calls itself?'

'Yeah! That's just who I mean.'

'So go to them,' Burgenhof challenged. 'Even if their enforcers, if you still call them that, should manage to locate Hippolyta and me, it certainly won't be to your advantage.'

'Maybe I'll take a chance on that,' Mabel threatened.

'Go ahead. Your employers are strong on the profit-motivation, I should imagine, and won't be averse to making a quick buck. I'm a wealthy man—'

'And you think you could buy them off?'

'More than that,' Burgenhof purred, sounding more sinsister than Peter Lorre playing one of his spine-tingling horror roles. 'We could buy permission to make another movie, with the same cast. Hippolyta would be delighted with the opportunity. Only this time you wouldn't come out of it so lightly.'

'*Lightly!*' Mabel squealed, left hand fluttering towards her battered features. Then the full implications behind 'Mark's' words struck her. 'God! You mean you'd—'

'We'd arrange to hire your services again,' Burgenhof confirmed.

'The Syndicate wouldn't buy that!' Mabel bluffed.

And was called.

'Wouldn't they, if the price was right?' the man mocked. 'And, as an inducement, we'd tell them that we paid you a whole lot more than five hundred dollars. I should think the Syndicate gets up-tight with girls who try to short change them.'

That, as Mabel knew all too well, was too mild a description of how her employers reacted when a hooker tried to turn in less than the correct amount of money. She had seen what happened to a couple who had been foolish enough to make the attempt. If the Syndicate accepted 'Mark's' lie, taken with an offer to pay well for the right to use her again, they would agree and count anything that happened to her as punishment for her 'disloyalty'.

'You lousy son-of-a-bitch!' Mabel said bitterly, in the tone of one who conceded that she was beaten.

'Call me names, if it makes you feel any better,' Burgenhof replied. 'Then bag your head and listen. None of your injuries are of a permanent nature. In a few days, all traces of them will be gone.'

'So?'

'Don't interrupt me, damn you! Hear me out. It's for your own good. Hippolyta and I were most satisfied with your performance last night. To show our appreciation, we have given you a bonus. You'll find another two hundred and fifty dollars in the envelope by the telephone. The charm bracelet in your handbag has company. Two diamond rings.'

'Wha – What—?' Mabel could only gobble incoherently.

'Look at them and have a long think about what I've said before you decide to try and have us located,' Burgenhof advised and something in the timbre of his voice sent a shiver through the girl. 'After all, much as Hippolyta loves to fight, I doubt if you share her enthusiasm. You *know* that the Syndicate would accept my proposition.'

'All right already,' Mabel groaned. 'You've sold me on it. Hey! Are you putting me on about the bonus?'

'Look and see,' Burgenhof instructed. 'By the way, I'll mail you the photographs as I promised. Goodbye, Mabel. Let's hope for your sake that we don't meet again.'

With that last cryptic utterance, the man hung up. After the line had gone dead, Mabel remained seated and staring dazedly at the receiver for several seconds. Replacing it, she gathered up the two envelopes, clicked on the apartment's lights and limped painfully back to the bed. Lowering her rump gingerly on to the mattress, she squinted through the slit of her right eye at the reflection in the mirror.

The bastards! That lousy pair of weirdo bastards! Well, no matter what 'Mark' had said, they were not going to get away with working her over.

Or were they?

Most of the hooker's instincts and inclinations revolted against the idea of lodging a complaint with the police. The Syndicate would not take a kindly attitude to her bringing the law into the affair. On top of that, the whole incident had been so strange and unlikely that she might find the badges reluctant to accept her story. They might think that she was lying to cover something up.

Even if the police believed her, they would need something to go on before they could locate 'Mark' and his wife.

Mabel tried to decide just how much information she could supply and was surprised to realize just how little it would be.

From what 'Mark' had told her, he was aware that she had memorized the Jeepster's licence number. So he must have spoken the truth when he claimed that it would not help in tracing him. Of course, there could not be too many vehicles of that make and colour around Gusher City. Perhaps the police could make use of that slender fact.

The pair's descriptions would be of far greater assistance. Unfortunately Mabel found herself unable to come up with exact details. If it came to a point, she found herself unable to recollect just what Mark looked like. Below average height, certainly, and with mousey brown 'hair-coloured' hair, but nothing more came to mind. All notions of him being a small, meek-looking, inoffensive and puny figure had departed during the time she had spent in the basement.

While Mabel had seen more than enough of Hippolyta, she doubted if she could mention one physical feature that would help the investigating officers to identify the woman. That shortish, curly tawny hair might narrow the field, but not sufficiently to make searching for her on the strength of it practical. Possibly Hippolyta's face would show bruising, if not to as great an extent as the girl's features. The marks would be noticeable, but only if the police could find the woman and see them. From all appearances and what 'Mark' had said, he was sufficiently wealthy for his wife to have no need to go out to work. So she could remain at home until all traces of her injuries had faded away.

How would the Syndicate react if they learned what had happened? Maybe they would look for the people responsible for her condition. Should they be successful – 'Mark' had warned her what would happen.

Picking up the envelope which she had addressed to herself, Mabel tore open its flap. The money was there, just as it had been when she sealed it in. An examination of the second envelope and her handbag proved that 'Mark' had spoken the truth about her 'bonus'.

Seven hundred and fifty dollars, two rings worth maybe a couple of hundred dollars and a golden charm bracelet that would bring in fifty bucks from a pawnbroker. Not a bad price for a collection of bruises and minor abrasions. Like 'Mark' had hinted, locating him and his wife would be anything but easy. And if she caused it to happen, she could easily wind up being the one who regretted it. The man had been correct in his claim that there would be no trace of her injuries in a few days. She was due for a period in the next couple of days, too. By the time she was clear, the bruising would have gone sufficiently for her to be back in business.

Close to a thousand dollars, less the Syndicate's cut – she decided not to take chances and declare the full amount of her earnings – was not a bad pick up. She could call the Bucket of Blood and tell Larry that she would not be around until Saturday and had a good enough record for it to be accepted without question. There was enough food in the apartment to last her until the marks would be less noticeable. Nobody, except the three people concerned, would ever know what had happened on Tuesday night. To hell with that kookie pair. If she never saw them again, it would be too soon.

Lowering herself to lie on the bed, Mabel gave a little groan. Despite the money it had brought her, she wished that 'Mark' had gone into Marty's Grill and picked up Della Zekov instead of coming to her.

At about the time that Mabel was reaching her decision to forget the Burgenhofs, Woman Deputy Alice Fayde and her partner, Deputy Sheriff Bradford Counter, were walking out of the D.P.S. Building. They left by the front entrance, crossed Randal Street and collected Alice's Ford Mustang from the municipal employees' parking lot.

There was a good reason for the deputies' decision to use a privately-owned vehicle instead of the distinctively marked Unit S.O. 12, which was their official conveyance. Three of the criminals named by I.C.R. had left their previous last-known-locations. There was a possibility that one had come to Gusher City. Alice and Brad were going in search of information. Official sources had failed to supply it, so they intended to make a round of their informers.

In view of the delicate nature of their work – gathering

and selling information about criminals to interested parties – stool pigeons naturally had an aversion to being visited by people who openly advertised that they were peace officers. Fully aware of the penalty of being caught informing, Alice and Brad had no desire to jeopardize the safety or secrecy of their unofficial sources of information.

All through the previous afternoon and evening, almost up to midnight, Alice, Brad, Joan and Cuchilo had been constantly on the move.

The blonde and her Comanche partner had visited the Euro-Tex Clothing Company in the hope of discovering a motive for Amy Willer's death, or some connection between the two victims. The hope had not materialized. They had learned nothing other than what they already knew, that Amy Willer was a loner who had a compulsion for gambling. There was no hint of her having had an affair, or even a friendship with any of the company's male employees. Emily Cochran had never been employed at Euro-Tex and Amy had worked there since graduating from Cardell University.

Calling at the bookstore where Emily had worked, Alice and Brad met with no greater success. The manager claimed that he had never seen Amy and knew little about Emily's private affairs. According to him, his employee had been her usual self on the day of her death and had not showed any signs of being worried or concerned.

Going to the movie theatre, the redhead and blond giant had gathered only negative information. The manager recognized Emily's picture and said that he had seen her in the foyer early the previous evening. An usherette had supplied the reason for Emily's early return home. Seeing the girl sitting alone, she had become involved in conversation and learned that Emily's date had failed to make an appearance. According to the usherette, the girl had been more annoyed than distressed by the man's non-arrival.

The rest of the watch had been spent by the two teams tracking down and interviewing Emily's friends and acquaintances. Although these had included the man who had failed to keep the date, nothing new or helpful had emerged. The man had been kept working late at his office and was unable to contact Emily to inform her. Like all the others, he proved to have an unshakeable alibi for the time of her death.

Intermingled with the other calls, the deputies had located and interviewed the four men in Gusher City to whom Glam-Batt had sent illustrated brochures. In each case, the man concerned had given a satisfactory account of his movements on Monday night. All but one had been able to produce his copy of the brochure intact. The fourth man had loaned his brochure to yet another girl fight *aficionado*. What might have been a hopeful lead petered out quickly. On arrival at the fifth fan's residence, they had discovered that he had the brochure and an alibi.

Guessing correctly that the brochure had a bearing on a serious crime, the fifth man had made a suggestion. He had produced his collection of *Pussy-Grapple* magazines. The booklets were devoted to the subject of women fighting with each other and carried extensive correspondence sections. Offering to lend Alice and Brad the magazines, he had pointed out that they might find letters from people living in Texas. If the killer was interested in the subject, he might have corresponded at some time. While Alice and Brad had felt that this was unlikely, they had accepted the offer. It might be a very, very, long shot; but so was much of deductive law enforcement.

Dealt with by the Sheriff's Sub-Office nearest to their respective homes, the remaining pair of *Glam-Batt* subscribers had established their innocence.

While the four deputies had been conducting that line of inquiry, a massive dragnet had been put out by the G.C.P.D. Every known mugger and other criminals with records of violent robbery who could be located had been picked up and delivered to the D.P.S. Building. Members of the Sheriff's Office had interrogated them on their arrival. The net result had been five confessions by men guilty of less serious crimes and who could not otherwise explain their whereabouts at the times of the killings. Nothing had come of the effort to help bring the peace officers closer to a solution to the two murders.

About the only bright aspect had been that the killer did not strike on Tuesday night.

Arriving at the D.P.S. Building on Wednesday morning,

Alice and Brad had not been too surprised to meet Joan in the front hall, or at finding Cuchilo in the squadroom. After logging on, the four deputies had held a conference on what little had been learned and to settle their next line of action. There had also been the m.c.'s necropsy report to read.

In the blunt, chillingly informal manner of such documents, it was stated that the cause of death in each case had been injuries inflicted on the skull by a round, possibly metal object. The girls had been struck repeatedly from the front, even after there must have clearly been no further need to continue the attack. The autopsies had established that neither girl was sexually assaulted before the attack. Nor had there been signs of pregnancy, or a successful abortion in either case. Negative information again, the latter discovery was useful in that it removed two possible motives for the killings.

Before the two teams could leave, First Deputy McCall had brought them an assignment. The previous evening, Jack Tragg had interviewed Fred and ordered the floorwalker to put him in touch with the senior member of the gambling organization. On Fred complying, the sheriff had made a request to which the boss had agreed. So the four deputies had left to keep an appointment. At a house on the borders of Gusher City South and Evans Hill, they had met the assembled staffs of the organization's card and dice games. Although the majority of the crowd had identified Amy Willer from her photograph, none could remember ever having seen Emily Cochran at a game.

More than ever, the four deputies had been inclined to believe that there was no connection between the girls. That left them with the probability that they had been victims of the same robber. The problem remaining was how to find the man who had committed the crimes.

Neither the Hollywood nor the Houston Police Departments' reports had arrived. However, the various other replies to I.C.R.'s request for information had come in. Although it was a long chance, Joan had suggested that the deputies should try asking around their informers regarding the possibility of one of the men who had not been accounted for having come to Gusher City.

At half past four, half an hour after they should have logged off watch, Alice and Brad reluctantly gave up their attempts. Since leaving the squadroom, they had contacted all their informers. The quest had not been successful. Returning to the D.P.S. Building, they found that Joan and Cuchilo had just arrived from an equally abortive mission.

'If any of those three are in town, they're not showing themselves,' Joan groaned, flopping into a chair at her team's desk. 'None of our informers have heard a whisper.'

'Or ours,' Alice admitted, taking the seat which Cuchilo indicated and kicking off her shoes. 'All we learned is that Mabel Liebeck and Della Zekov are feuding since Della moved into Marty's Grill.'

'That's on the same alley as the Bucket of Blood and nearer to The Street,' Joan remarked. 'No wonder Mabel's up-tight about it. Maybe we should have the blue-noses go down and tell them to keep the fussing off the streets.'

'I'd say they both know that,' Alice commented.

'Hey,' Brad drawled, bringing a chair from his team's desk. 'Why not call the Baxters. They might know a few more of these girl fight nuts.'

'Who're they?' Joan demanded.

'A couple over in Presidio County,' Alice replied. 'We met them on the Fairey Manders case.* They train girl wrestlers and Manders worked for them. Tom and Bubsy are all right guys. They'll help us if they can.'

'Do you reckon that there's anything in this girl fight bit?' Cuchilo inquired. 'As a lead in the case, I mean.'

'That piece of the brochure's just about the only lead we've got,' Joan pointed out. 'I'm betting that the killer dropped it. Could be that's what's going to take us to him.'

'I don't reckon those *Pussy-Grapple* magazines are going to be of much help,' Alice commented. 'I skimmed through a few of them last night. None of the letters have addresses, just names, or initials and a town.'

'According to Mac McCall,' Joan reminded the redhead, '*your* watch doesn't need any more than that to go on.'

'I'm too bushed to come up with a snappy answer,' Alice groaned. 'Did *you* read any of them?'

* Told in *The Deputies*.

'A couple,' Joan admitted. 'Some of those letters are way out. I reckon they were written by the fellers who publish the books. There was one that was a dilly. Some gal calling herself "Hippolyta", writing from an army base, described a fight she'd had with another W.A.C. If it was true, it would have made some of the brawls in Great-Grandpappy Mark's memoirs look like scuffles in a kindergarten's playground. Then she suggested that boxing should be part of the W.A.C.'s, W.A.V.E.'s and W.A.F.'s physical training curriculum, and that they should hold inter-service tournaments.'

Brad grinned at the reference to a book of his great-grandfather's memoirs which had been published. In his time, Mark Counter had witnessed and in some cases been the cause of memorable brawls involving various famous female personalities of the Old West.*

' "Hippolyta",' Cuchilo remarked. 'Wasn't she the queen of the Amazons in Greek mythology?'

'That's her,' Joan confirmed. 'And I'm betting that's what the "Hippolyta" in *Pussy-Grapple* is, a myth.'

'Or a "myth-is",' Alice drawled, then after the disgusted comments on the pun had died down, went on, 'But I go with you, Joan. I don't think she exists outside the minds of the *hombres* who write and publish the magazine.'

* Some of the incidents are told in *Quiet Town* (the battle in Bearcat Annie's saloon); the 'Bounty On Belle Starr's Scalp' and 'The Kidnappers' episodes in *Troubled Range* (Belle Starr and Calamity Jane, Cattle Annie and Little Britches); the 'The Gamblers' episode in *The Wildcats* (Poker Alice and Madame Moustache).

CHAPTER NINE

Cruising along the winding, hilly approach to Coolridge Avenue, holding his Plymouth sedan to a sedate thirty miles per hour, Oscar Burgenhof found himself speculating – as he had on other occasions – upon the identity of the man who had built the house in which he and Hippolyta now lived. It might have been erected with their specialized interests in mind.

To the west of his home, the road passed between the sheer, high walls of a draw. The houses along the top of each side had tall fences to prevent the occupants' children from reaching the dangerous edges. At the Coolridge Avenue end of the draw, curving to the right, the left hand wall extended perhaps two hundred yards further than its mate. Once beyond the extension, the road swung to the left.

Burgenhof's house was the first building on the right side. It had been erected at such an angle that its eastern end concealed the driveway and garage door from the view of the properties to the east, while the end of the draw hid them from the western properties. Provided that he took a little care, it was possible for him to drive in and out of the garage undetected. By the time his vehicle came into the neighbours' range of vision, there was nothing to suggest that it had not driven the full length of the Avenue or – depending on the direction in which he was travelling – through the draw.

All in all, despite having seriously depleted the couple's joint bank account, the house in Leander Division's high-rent Coolridge Avenue had already proved to be good value for the money. Burgenhof felt certain that it would continue to do so.

There was not even the danger that the neighbours might recognize Burgenhof as he drove by and become puzzled, or suspicious, by his comings and goings at unusual hours of the night.

Burgenhof possessed a quality of inconspicuousness which he found invaluable in his second, secret way of life. During the six weeks he and his wife had lived on Coolridge Avenue, few of their neighbours had made more than a nodding acquaintance with them. That had been part of the couple's policy. How well it had worked showed in that several neighbours had passed Burgenhof without recognizing him; both in the Business Division where he worked and closer to home. Except in the right circumstances, he bore such a negative personality that it was possible for him to be forgotten within minutes of his being introduced.

That could have explained why he did not hold a more important position with the great Houston Steel Products Corporation. The company's top brass knew him to be an excellent cost accountant, but he had never appealed to them as executive material. Nor did his wife do anything physically or socially to help him ascend the promotion ladder. Dull, uninteresting, dowdy of appearance, she was suspected of holding him back rather than moving him forward.

Being passed by in the promotion stakes had not embittered the Burgenhofs. It had almost seemed that neither of them had any ambition to go higher. So his application to be transferred to the Gusher City office had been granted without argument. Why he should have wished to do so, reducing still further his chances of advancement, might have aroused speculation but, to be truthful, few people in Houston had noticed that he was gone.

The Homicide Bureau of the Houston Police Department might have become indirectly aware of his departure, but they had never been actively conscious of his presence in the city.

Making the right hand turn which Mabel had noticed the previous night, the man guided his car across the sidewalk, down the slight incline and halted outside the garage. Its automatic door opened to let the Plymouth through and sank down again after the vehicle had entered.

Parking alongside the Jeepster station wagon, Burgenhof

switched off the Plymouth's engine. He climbed out and studied the other vehicle. Trust Hippolyta to have wasted no time. Since he had left for work that morning, she had removed the set of licence plates which Mabel might have memorized and locked them in a drawer of the work-bench prior to a more permanent disposal. From what she had said, when he called her on the telephone to tell of his conversation with the hooker, Hippolyta had also been busy developing the still photographs he had taken. He was waiting with eager anticipation to discover how they had come out.

Good for Hippolyta – that was not her baptismal name, but he never thought of her in any other way – what a help she was to him. In fact, he felt that the most fortunate single incident in his life had been meeting her.

The introduction had come while he was completing his draft service in the Army. A subscriber to *Pussy-Grapple* magazine, he had read with considerable interest a letter describing a boxing bout between the writer and another girl. To his surprise, it had been signed *'Hippolyta, Camp Logan, Missouri'*, the base at which he was stationed. However, with around two thousand officers and enlisted personnel on the base, locating the writer had appeared to be an impossibility. And, if he had succeeded, would he be fortunate enough to strike up an acquaintance?

All too well Burgenhof had known of his lack of attraction for the opposite sex. Despite his athletic prowess – that small frame packed surprising muscular development and strength – his general appearance had always prevented girls from taking him seriously. Not even his holding rank of captain in the Quartermaster's Corps and representing the base in pistol shooting competitions had changed the situation.

Luck, rather than deduction, had brought Burgenhof into contact with 'Hippolyta'. Entering the officers' club earlier than usual one day, he had seen the kind of unmarked – but to its devotees, familiar – envelope in which *Pussy-Grapple* was sent through the mail. Picking it up, he had found that it was not his copy, but addressed to a Lieutenant Grindale of the Women's Army Corps. Replacing the envelope, he had waited until its owner came to collect it and then introduced himself.

At first Hippolyta had been cold and distant, in the manner which had caused some of Burgenhof's brother officers to label her a lesbian. Once she had become convinced that he matched her own absorbing fascination for watching or reading about women fighting, she had soon proven that she was no dyke. From that day on, Hippolyta and Burgenhof had become practically inseparable. They married as soon as they had both left the service.

In their search for material on their subject, which they discovered stimulated their passions as nothing else could, the couple had attended movies which featured girl fights and purchased material from companies dealing in their interest. Always the obvious faking of the commercially-made home movies had disappointed and annoyed them. A physical fitness fanatic, Hippolyta had repeatedly declared that she could put on a more realistic display given the opportunity. Nothing had come of her suggestion until Burgenhof had been employed in a well-paid position with the Houston Steel Products Corporation.

That had been when they decided to make their own movies. There had been a number of snags to the idea. Finding opponents for Hippolyta had been one. Only a woman with a most desperate need for money would have been willing to take part in the kind of fighting Hippolyta planned on doing. Nor would they be likely to find opponents with pretty faces and decent figures disposed to take part, no matter how great the financial inducement. On the first few occasions, they might have been able to hire raddled hags, or bargain-price hookers. Even if they had been willing to settle for such unworthy assistance, the supply would rapidly dry up once word began to get around of what acceptance would entail.

Producing the films, still and movies, would have proved simple compared with the difficulty of finding opponents. When the couple had decided upon making their own girl fight material, they had joined a camera club to learn how to do so. By being able to print and develop their own films, they could eliminate the danger of allowing outsiders to learn what they had been doing.

After long hours of discussion, the Burgenhofs had finally

evolved what they had regarded as the solution to their problem. However, the cost of putting it into operation had proved to be high. By the time they had purchased all the necessary equipment – the custom features of the Jeepster had been expensive, but inescapable – they had lacked the funds to go ahead.

That difficulty had been solved. With two movies completed, using the unwilling help of hookers, the Burgenhofs had run into a dangerous snag. So dangerous, in fact, that they had decided to leave Houston. The move had been made and Burgenhof felt, in view of the previous night, that it had been worth while. There had, however, been the risk that the Houston victims had reported what happened to their bosses, despite the warnings they had been given. If so, news of the Burgenhofs' activities might have reached Gusher City. Mabel's acceptance of the story which had lured the other hookers indicated that this was not so.

Having checked that the garage's main entrance was locked, Burgenhof entered the basement. While crossing to the door through which his wife had made her appearance last night, a sense of libidinous satisfaction crept over him. At last Hippolyta and he had a girl fight movie of the kind they had always hoped for. Neither of the hookers in Houston had given anywhere near as lengthy and active participation as Mabel had produced. No commercial company's inept, obvious fakes could come even close to the kind of dramatic action the couple now had on film.

Leaving the basement, Burgenhof went swiftly up a flight of stairs. He felt the familiar tingle of anticipation which he always experienced when he was about to see some new material.

'I'm home, darling,' he called as he emerged in the ground floor's hall.

'In the kitchen, dear,' his wife replied.

Closing the door under the stairs leading to the first floor, through which he had just come, Burgenhof turned his feet in the required direction. Going to the rear of the house, he entered the kitchen.

It was the Mrs. Burgenhof always seen by the neighbours who rose from the table and came to greet him. Apart from the bloody nose, her face had not been marked during the fighting. Even the reddening left by Mabel's slaps in the second session had faded from the woman's bronzed cheeks. Dressed in a shapeless, dowdy frock and the unflattering mousey brown wig, she looked nothing like the magnificently developed savage of the previous night.

'Did you have a good day, dear?' Hyppolyta inquired, returning to the table and pouring him a cup of coffee.

'No different than usual,' Burgenhof replied, sitting down. His eyes darted restlessly around the room, searching for something. 'And you?'

'Pretty good,' Hippolyta answered. 'By the way, dear. I think we should fire the maid. She's much too inquisitive. Just this morning I told her not to go near the dark-room as I had some negatives drying—'

'She didn't get in and spoil them?' demanded Burgenhof, a hint of alarm in his voice.

'No,' Hippolyta assured him and her whole being seemed to exude a chilling menace. 'If she had, you wouldn't need to fire her. The door was locked, but I'm certain I almost caught her trying to peep through the keyhole when I went upstairs.'

'She takes too much interest in our mail, too,' Burgenhof remarked. 'And in what's thrown in the waste paper bin. You're right, dear. She'd better go.'

'I'll not bother hiring a replacement,' Hippolyta declared. 'She got paid as a maid, but she was never more than a cleaning woman.'

'Er—!' Burgenhof put in, unable to restrain his impatience any longer. 'Did you find time to make any prints from the negatives?'

'Of course I did,' the woman smiled, rising and crossing to unlock and open a drawer. She returned carrying an envelope. 'I had to put them there. That damned Mrs. Higgert and her Welcome Wagon clique have been round, collecting old clothes for something or other. I had to go and get some to get rid of them and we didn't want *her* laying hands on these, did we?'

Almost snatching the envelope from his wife's hand, Burgenhof extracted and started to study the photographs it held. Breathing a touch heavier, Hippolyta bent to look over his shoulder. The first photographs showed the woman applying a boston crab hold to Mabel. Other pictures of various wrestling grips and throws followed, including the pose which Mabel had remembered most vividly. In it, the two women stood face to face, each with her hands gripping and crushing at the other's breasts. While Mabel's face was twisted in an expression of agony, Hippolyta's features showed a kind of ecstatic pleasure at the pain. There were four photographs of that particular hold, the last being after the hooker had fainted through the torment. Six more shots depicted Hippolyta standing or kneeling astride the unconscious Mabel in postures of victory. The last two, inspired by the fade out to the fight sequence between Ginger Rogers and Iris Adrian in the 1942 movie *Roxie Hart*, had Hippolyta feigning unconsciousness and sprawled across the girl's supine body.

'I like the double k.o. shots, dear,' Burgenhof remarked. 'We should take more of them.'

'Yes, they are good,' Hippolyta agreed. 'We'll try to fake it in at the end of a movie fight, too.'

'That's a good idea. I don't suppose there's any way we could make it happen like it did in *Roxie Hart*?'

'We could always ask Mrs. Higgert to help us,' Hippolyta suggested with a grin. 'But I don't see her in the part of the matron who our fight disturbs so much that she bangs our heads together.'

'Or me,' Burgenhof smiled. 'But I'd like to see her face if we did ask. That was a neat way they ended the fight in *Roxie Hart*, though.'

'Wasn't it just! It's a pity all movie fights don't end so decisively.'

Instead of continuing to discuss the relative merits of the many fights between women in the movies they had seen, Burgenhof turned his attention to the 'double knock out' photographs. In them, Hippolyta appeared to have two black eyes and much more damage to her face than Mabel had inflicted.

'You did a good job with this make-up, dear,' he praised.

'It sets the final touch to them. You look as badly marked as she is.'

'My marks washed off,' Hippolyta reminded him. 'Do you think that she will keep quiet about what happened?'

'I think she will. I made a detour by her place on my way home. The drapes were still closed and that newspaper you leaned between them and the window was still in place. So I found a phone booth and called her in a disguised voice. She said she wouldn't be available for business until Saturday.'

'It certainly looks as if she is going to forget about us.'

'Yes. If she'd told anybody, they would have probably called in a doctor, or at least opened the drapes when they visited her. I don't think they'd have closed them and put the paper back. They wouldn't expect us to check up on her.'

While agreeing, Hippolyta changed the subject. Taking up one of the photographs, she held it where her husband could see it.

'This breast-claw sequence is good,' she remarked and her body wriggled in ecstatic recollection of the pain the hooker's fingers had caused to her bosom. 'Oscar! How soon can we shoot another movie?'

'That depends on you, dear,' Burgenhof replied.

'Let's not wait too long,' Hippolyta requested. 'Something could go wrong. The Syndicate might learn what happened. Or she might warn her friends.'

'That's possible,' Burgenhof agreed. 'Although I feel sure that she took my warning to heart and won't say a word about us.'

'Her friends might visit her when she doesn't show up on The Street—'

'I can always go to Green Park and pick up a girl—'

'Didn't you say something about having seen a blonde on The Street who was built as well as Liebeck?' Hippolyta interrupted.

'Yes. But she wasn't around last night.'

'Why not go and see if she is tonight?'

'*Tonight*?' Burgenhof yelped.

'Why not?' his wife demanded.

'It's you I'm thinking about, dear,' Burgenhof replied. 'Are you fully recovered from last night?'

'I've never felt better, darling,' Hippolyta assured him. 'I've a few bruises, but nothing to worry about. After I've softened her up with the boxing gloves, she won't give me any trouble for the rest of the action.'

'That's true,' Burgenhof conceded, being aware of how much advantage his wife gained from her skill as a boxer. 'Can we afford it?'

'We can scare up another seven hundred and fifty, with the remainder of your take on Monday night. There are enough pieces of jewellery left over for another girl.'

'Why the hell couldn't that bitch be carrying all her winnings in the handbag?' Burgenhof snapped pettishly, thinking about the story in the newspapers, telling how the killer of Amy Willer had overlooked several thousand dollars hidden in her car. 'If she had been, we'd be sitting pretty.'

'You couldn't be expected to know that she was carrying so much money,' Hippolyta replied soothingly. 'There was never more than fifteen hundred on any of them in Houston. It's unfortunate that you had to kill them both, dear.'

'They both turned and had a good look at me, so I thought it was for the best,' Burgenhof answered, lowering his head so that his wife would not see the evasive glint in his eyes. 'One of them might have given the police an accurate description of me. Anyway, the Sheriff's Office are most likely wasting time looking for a connection between them.'

'Nobody saw you, apart from the girls?'

'Nobody who was close enough to identify me. I was using that Mustang I'd picked up on the edge of Mockingbird Grove, so the law can't make my car.'

'By the way, dear,' Hippolyta remarked, changing the subject. 'I ran off three prints from each negative. Why don't we send one set to *Pussy-Grapple*?'

'Why not,' Burgenhof agreed. 'We can use an assumed name and have the reply put through a box number at the post office. Pictures like ours might shake Glam-Batt up and make them put out some of the same quality.'

'Not quite the same quality,' Hippolyta protested. 'They won't have our advantages.'

'I suppose not,' Burgenhof grinned. 'You might put up another set for Mabel. I promised we'd send her some of the prints. They'll serve as a reminder of what happened, and what might happen again if she gets the Syndicate after us.'

'Do you think they would let us use her again, if they found us?'

'Mabel thinks they would, and she knows them.'

'If all else fails, we could always try to contact her bosses,' Hippolyta suggested.

'I wouldn't want them knowing that much about us,' Burgenhof replied. 'Besides, I think it's more fun this way.'

'So do I,'smiled Hippolyta. 'Let's go upstairs and look at the photographs again, shall we?'

'I don't know,' Burgenhof answered. 'Perhaps we should keep our strength up for tonight.'

'So who's proved it's weakening?' challenged his wife. 'Anyway, you don't think I'll have any trouble in taking that blonde hooker. Do you?'

CHAPTER TEN

It was fortunate for the Burgenhofs that their basement was completely sound proof. Despite her masochistic gratification at having pain inflicted upon her, Hippolyta was screeching at the top of her voice. In none of the other fights had she experienced anything like the agony that was caused by the battered, bloody, blonde hooker's teeth sinking into the side of her right breast.

Up to that point in the proceedings, everything had gone pretty much as the Burgenhofs had planned. On his arrival at the Bijou Grande's parking lot, the man had been able to obtain the same position for his Jeepster that he had used on his meeting with Mabel. He had kept a careful watch for any signs that the hooker had informed her employers of her fate. In his jacket pocket had been a snub-nosed Smith & Wesson Chief's Special revolver, but that precaution had not been necessary.

Going to the alley, alert for the first hint of danger, Burgenhof had not been kept waiting long before Della Zekov had made an appearance. It had been with a sense of anticipation that he had approached her. All the time he had been going through the by-play of pretending to represent a rich business executive with a desire for secrecy, he had watched Della for the slightest warning that she knew what was coming. All he had seen was a similar reaction to that Mabel had shown. Completely fooled by his acting, the blonde had displayed the same thinly hidden amusement and derision. She had made only a token objection to accompanying him on his terms.

At the parking lot, she had addressed the envelope containing her fee. Although she had insisted on placing it in the mailbox herself, Bergenhof had contrived to read and memorize her name and address. That had been necessary so that he and Hippolyta could return her to her home after they were through with her. With the money safe in the hands of Uncle Sam, Della had obediently entered the Jeepster's rear compartment and been transported to the house on Coolridge Avenue. For the added consideration of Emily Cochran's wristwatch and bracelets, the blonde had removed her white blouse, mock leather mini skirt, calf high boots and jewellery, then donned the boxing gloves. Already stripped and equipped for the fray – the boxing gloves having been fastened by her husband before he left to collect the girl – Hippolyta had made her appearance on cue.

Like her predecessors, Della had started by protesting and insisting that she did not intend to fight. She too had been compelled to defend herself as best she could. Goaded by desperation, the blonde had helped to give the Burgenhofs some reasonable action before she had been knocked out by the more skilful Hippolyta. She had been left where she had fallen while the couple had sated their erotically inflamed passions. Then they had revived her and prepared her for the next part of their programme.

In her weakened condition, Della had been no match for Hippolyta in the all-in fight. Nor had the blonde's chances been improved by the psychological effect of realizing that her opponent enjoyed being hurt. After a few minutes of feminine struggling, involving hair pulling, punching, slapping and kneeing, Della's struggles had diminished. Dragging the sobbing, all but defeated girl after her by the hair, Hippolyta had started to rise from the mat. It had been her intention to end the fight in some manner which would allow her to fake the double knock out.

Desperate to avoid further punishment, Della had writhed close to her antagonist and pressed her face against Hippolyta's torso. Red, searing agony had been blazing through the blonde's head as it seemed that whole chunks of her hair would be torn out by the roots. In a panic-stricken attempt to end the torment, she had clamped her teeth on to the closest, most protuberant portion of Hippolyta's body. Even in her terrified, exhausted state, Della had become aware of the woman's response to the bite. Instinct had caused the hooker to cling on with all the strength she could muster.

Shriek after agonized shriek burst from Hippolyta. Stripped to his shorts and sodden with perspiration, Burkenhof ignored his wife's predicament and continued to keep the camera's motor rolling. Throwing her head from side to side as if doing so would reduce the pain she felt, Hippolyta set about releasing herself. With her fingers still enmeshed in the tangled blonde hair, she started to draw her hands outwards. At the same time, the woman moved back as far as she could and rammed first left then right knee as hard as possible into Della's body. The combined attack caused the hooker to open her mouth. Giving a gasping screech of relief, Hippolyta braced herself. With a surging heave at the trapped hair, she raised Della from the mat and flung her across the room. Crashing backwards into the wall, the blond leaned against the hard surface as if pinned against it.

For a few seconds, Hippolyta stood on spread-apart legs, with her hands cupped under the injured breast. Blood oozed from the oval indentations, dribbling over her fingers. Suddenly her face twisted into lines of bestial rage. With a scream that was barely human in its timbre, she dashed across the mat. Staring in horror at the approaching figure, Della tried to plead for mercy. No words came. Nor could she make her tormented body respond to her will. She just leaned on the wall, wide open for whatever Hippolyta planned to do next.

On coming close enough, Hippolyta leaped feet first at the girl and plunged both hands into her hair. Unable to retreat and too weak to support the woman's weight, Della was bent double. As Hippolyta's back touched the canvas, she thrust upwards with her feet against Della's stomach. Propelled by the woman's powerful leg muscles, Della's feet left the mat. The hooker turned a half somersault in midair, alighting first and hard on the floor. Accompanied by a faint, but audible pop, she flopped rag doll limp on to her back some feet from her assailant.

Rising into a kneeling position and twisting around, Hippolyta flung herself towards the motionless girl. Straddling Della's unresisting torso with her knees, the woman grabbed her by the hair and raised then crashed her head on to the mat. Realizing that her victim was no longer struggling, Hippolyta released the hair. Resting her hand on Della's shoulders, she looked at her husband.

'Great, darling, just great!' Burgenhof enthused, stopping the camera and going to his wife's side. Placing his hands under her arm-pits, he raised her gently to her feet. 'Let me do something about that bite, then we'll shoot the victory poses.'

'Oh lord!' Hippolyta moaned, clutching at the bitten area. 'It hurts. How it hurts! I'll get even with her, Oscar. See if I don't.'

'So you will, dear,' Burgenhof agreed soothingly, helping his wife across to the table. 'You can do it when we take the still pictures.'

'She's quiet,' Hippolyta remarked, glancing at the blonde after the wound had been disinfected and had a pad of cotton wool taped over it to absorb the blood.

'Too quiet,' the man admitted, studying the motionless figure. 'She ought to be showing some signs of recovery by now.'

'Oscar!' Hippolyta ejaculated. 'She's not breathing!'

Darting forward, the man knelt at the blonde's side. As he noticed the manner in which her head was tilted, he guessed what had happened. To make sure, he took hold of her right wrist between his left thumb and forefinger, trying to locate the beat of her pulse.

'She must have landed badly and broken her neck,' he said in a matter of fact tone.

'We've always known that something like this could happen,' Hippolyta answered calmly, as if breaking another woman's neck was an everyday occurrence. 'There's nothing we can do about it now. We've got some good footage and can still shoot the victory poses before we get rid of her body.'

'Perhaps we should forget the victory poses this time, dear,' Burgenhof remarked, 'What time is it?'

Picking up the wristwatch Della had removed, along with her other jewellery when preparing to don the boxing gloves, Hippolyta looked at it and replied, 'Just after ten.'

'Then perhaps I'd better take her straight away. There's

less chance of being seen, remembered and maybe recognized before midnight.'

'That's true enough. Are you going to take her to her apartment?'

'I think not. There's a better place down in Gusher City South, on the industrial development area. Dixon pointed it out to me the morning he took me along to our plant for the first time.'

'Where is it?' Hippolyta insisted.

'A hollow in a vacant lot between two factories,' Burgenhof elaborated. 'From what Dixon told me, a car was left in it by the Colismides' gang after they'd used it in an attempt to kill a deputy sheriff's wife.* Apparently the bottom of the hollow can't be seen from the streets, or the surrounding properties, and the car shouldn't have been found for days.'

'But it was,' the woman guessed.

'Yes,' her husband admitted. 'In fact it was found very quickly, but only because the police were making a thorough search. That was only to be expected under the circumstances. They won't go to all that trouble just because a hooker is reported missing.'

'Probably not,' Hippolyta conceded. 'Anyway, once she's missed her bosses aren't likely to go to the police. Of course, she might be found by accident.'

'It's not likely to be tonight while I'm taking her, and after I've dumped her it will be too late for them to connect us to her. The alley was empty when I met her and I doubt if anybody will remember having seen us together.'

'If they do, I'll bet they'll not be sure of your description,' Hippolyta smiled, being fully aware of her husband's quality of anonymity. Then she lost her smile and said, 'How about the envelope you gave to her?'

'There's no way we can recover it, or for it to be traced back to us,' Burgenhof assured her. It's an ordinary commercial brand that sells in millions and so was the ball point pen I gave her to address it.'

'Your fingerprints are on the envelope,' Hippolyta warned.

* Told in *The ¼ Second Draw.*

'They'll probably be smudged, and are sure to have some company by the time it's passed through the mails and been delivered.'

'Why not take her outside the city limits and dump her?'

'Because I'd have to find the right kind of spot and I know how to reach that vacant lot.'

'You know best, dear,' Hippolyta said. 'Are you going to take her in the station wagon?'

'No,' Burgenhof decided. 'The Plymouth is less noticeable.'

'Go and dress then,' Hippolyta suggested. 'I'll get her ready to be moved while you're doing it.'

'Will you be all right, dear?' Burgenhof inquired solicitously. 'That was a bad bite she gave you and think you'll have a black eye by morning.'

'It feels that way,' the woman agreed, touching her left cheek gingerly with the tip of a finger. 'I didn't get to block one of her punches. But I'll be fine. After you've gone, I'll take a shower and rest until you get back.'

Leaving the basement, Burgenhof returned after about fifteen minutes. He was attired in his usual manner and once more looked the dapper little milksop. Incongruous with his appearance, a black Luger automatic pistol with an eight inch long barrel dangled from his right hand.

'You're taking the Luger?' Hippolyta asked.

'I prefer it to the snubbie,' Burgenhof replied. 'And there's no need for me to hide it under my jacket.'

The woman had wasted no time while her husband was dressing. Already she had dressed the dead girl and replaced the items of jewellery which Della had removed. Thrusting the Luger into his waistband, Burgenhof took hold of the blonde's shoulders. With his wife lifting the feet, the man carried the body across to the garage's entrance. Releasing her end of their burden, Hippolyta opened the door and clicked on the lights. Then they hauled the body to the Plymouth and laid it on the rear seat. Settling himself behind the steering wheel, Burgenhof placed the Luger on the adjacent passenger seat. He covered it with a newspaper he had purchased outside the office building and forgotten to take from the car.

'Perhaps you'd better go back into the basement before I leave, dear,' the man remarked as Hippolyta went to unlock the garage's front door. 'If anybody should happen to be passing and saw you like that—'

'It *would* start the neighbours talking,' Hippolyta chuckled, running her thumbs around the top of the white satin briefs which were still her sole item of clothing.

Operating the switch of the automatic locking and opening device, the woman turned and walked back to the basement's door. She waved her hand and passed through. Following her every movement with his eyes, Burgenhof ran the tip of his tongue across his lips in an anticipatory manner. Once he had disposed of the body and returned, they could make up for the time lost through Hippolyta's injury and the blonde's death.

On leaving the garage, Burgenhof paused long enough to make sure that its door had swung down into the closed position. Then he set the Plymouth into motion, turned east along Coolridge Avenue and drove at a sedate, law-abiding pace towards his destination.

Although the man had not been in Gusher City for any length of time, he already knew his way around as well as any long established resident. As part of his preparations for continuing with the movie production, he had studied street maps and driven hundreds of miles to familiarize himself with the terrain. The robberies were necessary to finance the productions, for the hookers were less likely to complain to the law or their bosses after being well paid. Before attempting to commit the crimes, he had wanted to locate areas which offered suitable victims. More important, he intended to be sure that he could always find an avenue of escape and avoid turning into a *cul-de-sac* if he should be pursued.

Nor had Burgenhof's precautions ended there. He was no fool, blindly accepting good fortune and leaving possible eventualities out of his considerations. All too well he had foreseen the dangers of producing the movies. Hippolyta possessed a working knowledge of boxing and judo, so she had been trained to fall and land safely when thrown. Unfortunately, her opponents would be unlikely to share her knowledge. Which meant that there had always been the risk of a fatal accident. Being a smart, careful man, Burgenhof had sought for a solution to that contingency.

From the first time Dixon – a member of the company assigned to acquaint Burgenhof with their interests in the city – had pointed out the hollow and told its story, he had been aware of its possibility as a dumping ground for a victim. So Burgenhof had selected the shortest route from his home to the vacant lot and studied it until he could almost have driven it with his eyes closed.

With his careful driving, Burgenhof attracted no attention from the few r.p. cars and foot patrolmen he passed during the journey to the vacant lot. On his arrival, he found the street deserted. That had been as he expected. On one side of the open ground was a plastic manufacturing company and, at the other, a footwear factory. Neither of them, nor the warehouse opposite, operated a night shift or strict security systems. Several reconnaissances had convinced him that he could make his delivery without being detected.

Halting the Plymouth, Burgenhof switched off all its lights. Waiting for a short time, just in case somebody had seen him and would come to investigate, he climbed out when they did not. Opening the rear door, he gripped the body under its arm-pits and hauled it on to the sidewalk. Making use of his powerful small body, he raised the burden until he could drape it across his right shoulder in a fireman's carry. Grunting a little under the weight, he started to walk over the hard, uneven surface of the lot. He had his arm between the dead girl's shapely legs, with her head and arms dangling loosely behind him. Della had been tall and her hands trailed on to the ground. Unseen by Burgenhof, the fancy paste-diamond bracelet she had been wearing came free and was left behind. Coming to the edge of the large hollow, Burgenhof snorted gratefully and dumped his burden over. As the body rolled to the bottom, he turned and hurried back to the car. Underfoot, the surface was rock-hard and he knew that he would not be leaving any footprints. Unless he was caught in the next few seconds, he would be gone without a trace.

In his haste to depart, Burgenhof did not see the bracelet on the ground.

Instead of returning home by the direct route, Burgenhof steered the Plymouth towards Lasher Division. He had two reasons for his actions, although he was only fully conscious of one of them. While he had decided that he might as well try to pick up another victim or two, he also had a subconscious desire to revisit the scenes of his crimes.

Going by the Willers' residence, the small man drew back his teeth in a tight, vicious grin. Like the Cochran girl earlier, Amy Willer had heard him approaching and turned to face him. Of course, neither girl had seen the Luger which he had held concealed behind his back. Their reactions had been almost identical. Despite being confronted by a stranger, neither had shown more than a momentary alarm over his unexpected arrival.

That, rather than any fear of being described to the police, was why Burgenhof had killed the two girls. Faced with a larger man, they would have been curious, frightened even. Instead, after a brief display of alarm, both had clearly dismissed him as harmless, or unworthy of serious attention.

Cold anger boiled inside Burgenhof as he continued to drive. All his life, women had sold him short. Because he was not big, or tough looking, they had regarded him as innocuous and beneath their consideration. Well, a few of them knew differently now.

All the time the thoughts had been boiling inside Burgenhof, his eyes had been working. He had seen a number of cars, but none which took his fancy. At last he found what he had been looking for. A Ford convertible, with its top open, crossed an intersection ahead of him. Its only occupant was a buxom, middle-aged blonde woman. Almost without the need for conscious thought, he swung the Plymouth on to the street behind the Ford.

A man could always learn from his mistakes. In Houston, Burgenhof had only asked that his female victim be alone; he had not bothered about the type of vehicle she drove. At first, that had worked out fine. Then he had picked on a woman apparently alone in a Chevrolet sedan. Although the vehicle had appeared to be carrying only one person, there had been a man asleep on its back seat. By the time that fact had become apparent, it was too late for Burgenhof to withdraw. He had just pistol-whipped the woman when the man had leapt from the car. Reacting instinctively, Burgenhof had turned and fired the Luger instead of using it as a club. Struck in the head, the man had gone down. Although dazed by his blow, the woman had started to scream. So Burgenhof had shot her between the eyes and silenced her.

Being certain that the police would put even greater effort into trying to locate him now that he had killed, Burgenhof had decided to get out of Houston. He had also promised himself that in future he would restrict his efforts to women driving convertibles with open tops. In that way, he could be reasonably sure that the victim was alone. Being in South-West Texas, especially in summer, Gusher City's climate was ideally suited to his needs. There were many convertibles on the streets and most of them had their tops open.

The street along which the blonde led Burgenhof was lined with apartment buildings. In the forecourt of one, an outdoor barbecue was in full session. Men and women in versions of cowhand clothing swarmed around the tables and the sounds of music and hilarity reached Burgenhof's ears. For a moment, he felt a twinge of annoyance. If the blonde was to join the revellers, she would be lost to him. However, although she looked at the forecourt in passing, she did not stop. Three buildings beyond the party, she signalled a turn. Luck favoured Burgenhof, for the parking lot she entered was on the end of the apartment house furthest from the barbecue.

Slowing down, Burgenhof saw the blonde bringing her car to a halt under the roof of an open-fronted garage. He braked the Plymouth, slipping the Luger from under the newspaper almost before the vehicle's forward movement had ended. Swinging on to the sidewalk, he placed both hands behind his back and strolled across the unlit parking lot. Already the blonde had left the convertible and was hanging a large shoulder bag over her left shoulder. Hearing his footsteps, she turned to look at him. She wore a dark trouser suit and had a good looking face which showed no surprise nor concern at finding him stalking purposefully out of the darkness towards her.

Burgenhof promised himself that he would rapidly make her regret her attitude regarding him.

CHAPTER ELEVEN

LIFTING the bulky Pete Ludwig bag from the front passenger seat of the Ford Convertible, Joan Hilton slung its carry strap over her left shoulder. On hearing the patter of footsteps, she turned and peered through the darkness outside the garage. Studying the approaching male figure, she felt a sensation of annoyance, starting to build up inside her. Since she had first walked a beat as a uniformed policewoman, the blonde had come to recognize the kind of symptoms she believed the small man was exhibiting. Going by his appearance and general bearing, he was a *most* law-abiding member of the community – and knew it.

In which case, Joan was certain that she could guess why he was stalking towards her. He advanced, peering with owlish determination through his glasses and with hands, like that limey Prince Philip, behind his back. His whole manner was suggestive of righteous indignation. That was the air of a tax-paying citizen on his way to demand that a female peace officer should attend to her duties – after all, he *did* help to subsidize her salary – instead of goofing off to her apartment.

That duty, of course, would be to go immediately along the street and order the folks at the barbecue to hold the noise down or knock it off altogether. Handling such a task hardly came under the jurisdiction of the Sheriff's Office; a fact which Joan knew all too well, but which was unlikely to influence the small, indignant, tax payer in his insistence that she should take some action.

Normally Joan would have been more tolerant. She had been a peace officer for long enough to have learned the value of maintaining good relations with members of the public. However, at that moment her sole ambition, aim and desire was to go straight up to her apartment. Once there, she would take a hot bath, climb into bed and knock off some uninterrupted and much needed sleep. So she had no intention of allowing a minor complaint – which, after all, should be, and could be, handled equally well by a Lasher Division radio patrol car – to ruin her hopes in that direction. Especially as she would be called out again if anything new should develop on her current case.

Despite the killer of Amy Willer and Emily Cochran having refrained from showing his hand on Tuesday night, the two deputy teams had not slackened their attempts to locate him. There had still been interviews to carry out and statements to recheck in the hope of picking up some thread of a clue that had been overlooked earlier.

Of all detective work, that was the kind which Joan had always disliked most. It was tedious, boring, time-consuming and in many cases, it led nowhere. Yet it had to be done in the hope that something would turn up, especially when other avenues of investigation stubbornly refused to present themselves.

More out of desperation than hope, the deputies had asked the Department of Motor Vehicles for information concerning all registered Ford Mustangs in the county, D.M.V.'s Auto Theft Detail had come back with a report of such a car, coloured seafoam green, being stolen on Monday night. It had been taken from a parking lot on the fringes of Lasher Division some time between eight and nine o'clock and was found at eleven on a street less than half a mile from the point of its disappearance.

Following their normal routine, Auto Theft had had the car examined thoroughly. Its ashtrays contained only butts of the type of cigarette smoked by its owner. The only fingerprints found had been accounted for. However, the owner had known what its mileage had been and there was an increase far beyond the distance at which it had been found. While the absence of unidentified fingerprints might have been thought a significant point, the Auto Theft detectives had pointed out that kids had long since become wised up to the danger of leaving such incriminating evidence when stealing a car to go joy riding.

Although criminals sometimes reported their vehicles

stolen, so as to establish an alibi for their activities in it, the deputies did not trouble to check up on the owner. According to Auto Theft, she was an elderly, white haired woman of sizeable proportions and could account for her movements through all the period the vehicle had been missing.

None of the four deputies' coterie of professional informers had come up with anything definite. On being called, four at least had claimed that the underworld was at a loss to identify the killer who had caused so much heat to descend on them.

Reluctantly, Joan and her companions had finally agreed that they were facing the one kind of criminal no peace officer cared to contemplate, much less try to catch: an utterly ruthless amateur. A bad *hombre* with no underworld connections that might lead to his location and arrest.

Having concluded that they were not dealing with a professional criminal whose face, fingerprints and identity were recorded in some law enforcement organization's files, the deputies had turned their attention to another aspect. According to the m.e.'s necropsy reports, each of the victims had been struck down by an assailant who had stood in front of her. Which implied that they had both allowed him to walk up without feeling the need to yell for help.

Why had the girls been so trusting?

Did it mean that they had both known the killer?

Or was it that each victim had believed that she had nothing to fear from the man confronting her?

If the latter should prove to be the answer, the killer must have been a man whom two girls with different social background and outlooks felt could be trusted. In Amy Willer's case, under the circumstances, there would have been few kinds of men who came into that category.

So the deputies had tried to select the kinds of men both girls would have accepted as harmless or trustworthy. The lateness of the hour precluded mail- or milkmen, while newspaper delivery boys could be discounted on the same grounds. A priest, or a rabbi would not be suspected – nor would a G.C.P.D. patrolman. With feelings of relief – for no decent peace officer cared to think about another lawman going bad – the deputies discounted the latter, as the witnesses would have remembered and commented on his uniform.

Joan had requested R. and I. to dig out the names of local criminals who had disguised themselves as priests, rabbis, or other church dignitaries while committing crimes. The abortive checking of the three names supplied had taken until nine o'clock in the evening. On the two teams returning to the deputies' squadroom, the Watch Commander had told them they could log off for the night.

Having put in many extra hours on the case, the four deputies had felt no twinges of conscience at obeying the order. They had eaten a meal together at the Badge Diner, then collected their cars from the municipal employees' parking lot and set off for their respective homes.

Although Joan had seen and heard the barbecue in passing, she had ignored it. The guests were celebrating the return of two young men who had just ended their service with the Green Berets in Vietnam. Figuring that the guests-of-honour deserved a celebration after what they had been through, she saw no reason to interfere.

Of course, she had realized that other people in the vicinity might not agree with her on the subject. Unless she now missed her guess, one of the dissenters was coming to lodge a protest and a demand for her participation. While she could not remember having seen him around the neighbourhood, he must have recognized her. That was the worst of driving a convertible with its top open—

An open-topped convertible!

Suddenly a warning started to ring in Joan's head.

Apart from the victims being unmarried women, they had had only one other thing in common. Like tonight, the weather had been warm and dry. So each of them had been driving her *convertible* with its top in the open position. That fact had been noted by the investigating officers and had explained how the killer had selected his victims.

Why had the girls kept quiet, instead of starting to scream for help at the sight of their assailant?

Because they had known him – *or had believed that he was harmless!*

Nobody could look more harmless or innocuous than that small, slim, inoffensive-seeming man. While he might believe that he was stalking impressively and authoritatively towards the woman deputy, he conveyed about as much menace as an English house sparrow picking up crumbs on a lawn.

Hell, he could not be the two girls' killer!

Would a mugger in search of another victim, seeing the distinctive bulk of the Pete Ludwig bag dangling from Joan's shoulder, continue with his attempt when faced by evidence that she was a female peace officer?

Joan had to admit that he might do just that. If, as the deputies suspected, he was an amateur without criminal connections, he might fail to understand the significance of the bag. While the Bureau of Women Officers issued them to all its members, they were not standard police equipment outside Rockabye County. So the man might not recognize the clue to her identity. Or if he should be committing the crimes for kicks rather than profit, a theory which had been discussed by the deputies, he would be unlikely to allow evidence of the blonde's official status to deter him. It might even form an added inducement for him to continue with his assault and robbery.

Assuming, that is, he was the killer and not merely an indignant tax payer coming to demand that Woman Deputy Hilton did her duty by stopping the noise made by the guests at the barbecue.

Glancing beyond the man, Joan felt as if an icy hand was running up and down her spine. A Plymouth sedan, dark in colour, stood empty just beyond the parking lot's gates. It had not been there when she had driven in.

Just about the only details the various witnesses in the Emily Cochran killing had agreed upon was that the man they had seen wore glasses and had arrived in a car of some kind shortly after the girl had turned into the driveway of her home.

A coincidence?

Maybe.

But if Joan made a wrong guess, it might easily get her killed.

The little man had entered the garage and was already much too close for comfort!

Seeing the change of expression which flickered across the buxom blonde's face, Burgenhof realized that, for some reason, she had revised her original opinion respecting his harmless appearance. Just how he could not guess, but she now figured that he was dangerous. It was a very satisfactory sensation to know that he had at least impressed a member of the opposite sex with his masculine superiority. He must consolidate his position quickly.

Springing forward, Burgenhof brought his arms from behind his back. The right hand, gripping the Artillery Model Luger, extended upwards. It whipped down again with lightning speed. That was the kind of attack he had launched against all his other female victims, smashing the eight inch barrel on to the top of each skull. Struck there, the blonde would either be knocked to the ground unconscious or so badly dazed that she would be unable to offer any resistance.

On each previous occasion, that was how things had gone. Combined with his sudden transition from a mild, inoffensive little milksop to a deadly menace, the sight of his long barrelled automatic pistol had invariably caused the women to freeze into immobility for long enough to make the attack successful.

The realization of her predicament had come to Joan just an instant too late. She had also underestimated the speed with which the small man would move. However, she had been partially expecting something of the kind and harboured no feminine fear of firearms. So she had already started to take evasive action.

Although Joan had thrust herself rearwards, she had not retreated far enough to carry her all the way clear of the blow. Coming down, the Luger's barrel missed striking the crown of her skull. Instead, its muzzle caught her on the forehead just below the hair-line at the left and raked across towards the brow of her right eye. Blood burst from the furrow carved by the round tube of steel.

Gasping in pain, Joan continued her withdrawal for a few steps. Although her head swam, she struggled to retain her balance for she knew that to go down would be fatal. Instinct and training was causing her to grip hold of the shoulder bag. Common sense guided her to open her mouth ready to scream as loudly as she could for help.

Showing the same rapidity of movement which had characterized his first blow, Burgenhof followed the staggering blonde. Once more he directed the barrel of his Luger in a sweeping arc towards her head. Instead of screaming, Joan devoted her breath and attention to self-preservation. Coming to a halt, she grasped the bottom of her bag in both hands and thrust it upwards. Interposing the bag between her head and the automatic, she halted the latter before it could reach its target. Still holding off the Luger, Joan pivoted from the hips and swung around her left leg. Bending it, she crashed the knee into Burgenhof's ribs. With a startled, pain-filled grunt, the little man pitched away from the blonde and across the garage.

Half blinded by the blood which flowed down her forehead, the woman deputy watched Burgenhof's involuntary departure. Cold logic warned her against following him. Before she could arrive, he would have halted and been ready to receive her. That short-grown bastard moved too fast for her to take unnecessary chances. So, remaining by the convertible, she tightened her grip on the bag with her left hand. Lowering it, she knocked open the flap and inserted her right hand. Never had the hard, checkered grips of the little Colt Cobra felt so good to her clutching fingers. Plucking the weapon from its holster, she started to draw it clear of the bag.

Coming to a halt, Burgenhof tensed, ready to charge back and resume his attack. He saw the black shape of the snub-nosed revolver emerging from the blonde's bag. Spitting out an ejaculation of surprise, he snapped the Luger into a waist-high instinctive alignment. As he sank automatically into a crouching posture behind the pistol, the heel of his left hand rose to thrust the safety catch upwards into the firing position. His every action, from the deft way he changed the setting of the safety catch to the manner in which he sank effortlessly into the kind of combat shooting crouch perfected for close range situations by the F.B.I., denoted considerable training and ability.

Still hampered by the running blood all but obscuring her vision, Joan tried to line the Cobra at her assailant. Even as her right forefinger began to tighten on the trigger, she formed a brief impression that a glow of flame was spurting in her direction from the little man. Sudden, raw agony blazed through her as something hot bored into her body. At that moment, she depressed the trigger sufficiently to let the mechanism release and propel forward the hammer. Even as the Cobra kicked wickedly in her grasp, she saw the Luger's second muzzle-blast glowing briefly and redly. Another burning sensation ripped at her nervous system as the 9mm bullet spiked into her torso just beneath her right breast.

With the sound of Joan's close-passing bullet still ringing eerily in his ears, Burgenhof saw his second shot strike her. Letting her bag fall from the left hand, but retaining her hold on the revolver, the blonde staggered in a half circle. As she stumbled against the side of the convertible, she hooked her left arm over its door and tried to hold herself erect.

For a moment fear bit at Burgenhof. He had never before heard the sound of a bullet splitting the air close to his head. It had been so unnerving that he almost turned and ran. Then he saw the woman staring at him with an expression of such concentrated hatred and fury that his fear grew greater. She was trying to line the revolver at him and again opening her mouth to either speak or scream.

'Bastard!' Joan croaked, agony preventing her from making better use of her voice. 'Little bastard!'

Probably nothing else could have jolted out the fear which was threatening to engulf Burgenhof. The words ripped through him like a red-hot knife. Despite all he had done to her, that *woman* still did not respect him. Twisting his features into a snarl, he darted towards Joan. The blonde saw him coming through the swirling pain mists which rolled about her. Desperately she tried to point the Cobra but her forefinger lacked the strength to squeeze its trigger. Leaping into range, Burgenhof slapped aside the little revolver and swung the Luger round-arm. Eight inches of steel impacted viciously against the side of the blonde's head and she went down as if she had been boned.

Spitting out a flow of obscenities, which few of his business associates would have credited him with knowing, much less uttering. Burgenhof kicked the motionless figure in the ribs. Bending, he gripped the shoulder of Joan's jacket in his left hand and dragged her torso from the garage's floor. Even as he raised the Luger to strike, he paused and stared across the parking lot.

At that moment, a sense of peril struck the small man. He realized that the entire incident could have been seen from the street, or by a chance onlooker in the buildings beyond it.

Beating a girl over the head in thick shadows, or inside an enclosed garage behind a darkened, clearly unoccupied house, had been safe enough. The blows had made little noise and neither victim had been granted the opportunity to scream. He and the blonde had been struggling in an exposed position and the sounds of the shots might have attracted attention. Even now, somebody might be calling the police or coming to investigate. So, much as he wanted to repay her for the disrespect she had shown, caution prevailed.

Releasing Joan, Burgenhof darted from the garage. He was halfway across the parking lot before he remembered the reason for his being there.

Should he go back and collect the blonde's shoulder bag?

A woman who toted a gun in her handbag might also be carrying a fair sum of money. After missing out on the Willer girl's concealed winnings, he had no wish to repeat his error. Yet to return might easily be his downfall. Regretfully, he concluded that he must keep going and forget any thoughts of profiting by the attack.

Gun in hand and alert for any warning that he had been detected, Burgenhof strolled rapidly to the Plymouth. Slipping behind the steering wheel, he slid the automatic under the newspaper on the other seat. Nobody challenged him, or tried to prevent him from driving away. Nor could he hear the sound of sirens approaching, with their warning that the attack had been seen and the police informed. His emotions were still churning wildly, but he forced himself to drive with his usual fussy attention to the traffic regulations. Nobody who might have happened to notice the Plymouth passing by would have imagined that it was being driven by a man fleeing from the commission of a serious crime.

Once clear of the Mockingbird Grove area, and safely on his way to Coolridge Avenue, Burgenhof allowed his thoughts to return to the blonde. He wondered who she was. Whoever, or whatever she might have been, she had known how to take care of herself in a tight corner. Such a woman would have made a worthy opponent for Hippolyta. If he could only have brought the blonde and his wife together in the privacy of the basement gymnasium, he felt certain that he would have filmed a fight far beyond anything an untrained hooker could put up.

CHAPTER TWELVE

AT half past eleven on Thursday morning, a swarthy, flashily-dressed, medium-sized Mexican stepped in a somewhat furtive manner out of Della Zekov's ground floor apartment. He had the appearance of a man with a guilty conscience and the desire to avoid being seen leaving. Turning along the hall towards the front door of the building, he came face to face with Woman Deputy Alice Fayde and her partner, Deputy Sheriff Bradford Counter. A startled exclamation burst from the man's lips and his right hand whisked under his jacket to where a Colt Cobra was holstered on the left side of his waist belt.

Although the man did not know it, he could blame Oscar and Hippolyta Burgenhof for the predicament in which he now found himself.

Almost an hour had passed before Joan Hilton's unconscious body had been discovered and news of the attack upon her had reached the Sheriff's Office. Few kinds of call received such prompt attention as when a peace officer had been the victim of an assault. Forgetting their intentions of logging off watch and going home, the deputies in the squad-room had immediately placed themselves at Alvarez's disposal. Knowing of the close friendship which existed between Joan and Alice, the Watch Commander had asked the G.C.P.D.'s Business Office to notify the redhead of the shooting. Sam Cuchilo had also been called with the news at his home.

The fact that Joan had been shot, instead of beaten on the head, and not robbed had led the sheriff and his deputies to an erroneous conclusion. None of them had connected the incident with the murders of Emily Cochran and Amy Willer. Instead, they had concluded that the blonde had been the victim of attempted revenge by some person with a grudge against her.

While some of the deputies had commenced a fruitless search for witnesses in the neighbourhood, Alice, Brad and the others had returned to the D.P.S. Building. There, they had checked through the Office's files and selected criminals who had reasons to hold a grudge against Joan. Working willingly to see what they could turn up, the skeleton night staff of the Records & Information Bureau had delved into cases on which Joan had worked before receiving promotion to deputy sheriff. By eight o'clock on Thursday morning, a list of possibles had been drawn up. Every deputy team of both watches who were not on an essential assignment had been detailed to help check out the alibis of the suspects.

Alice and Brad had been returning to the D.P.S. Building after interrogating a criminal in Gusher City South when they had been diverted to the vacant lot in which Burgenhof had dumped Della's body. With their county-wide jurisdiction offering greater freedom of movement than possessed by the municipal officers, the deputies of the Sheriff's Office combined acting as Gusher City's homicide squad with their other duties. That meant a team had to be sent to the scene of every unattended death.

On reaching their destination, Alice had recognized the victim. Seeing the bruised and battered state of the body, she had also remembered an item of news which had been supplied by an informer. So she had raised Central Control on the Oldsmobile's radio and asked that the Vice & Gambling Detail produce Della Zekov's and Mabel Liebeck's home addresses. While waiting for the answer, the deputies had learned how the dead hooker had been discovered. A patrolman walking his beat had seen the sun glinting on something in the vacant lot. Investigating as a matter of course, he had found Della's bracelet and had continued to the edge of the hollow. By doing so, he had ruined Burgenhof's hope that the corpse would remain undetected for several days.

Receiving the required information, Alice and Brad had set off to visit Mabel. As their route would take them by Della's apartment, the redhead had suggested that they should stop by and see if they could learn anything. Going by the Mexican's behaviour on seeing them, the deputies wondered if at last their luck had taken a turn for the better. Clearly the man resented their presence, which could mean that he might be Della's killer.

Not that the deputies devoted much time to considering the reason for the Mexican's actions. Their trained reflexes assessed the situation and came up with the answers, almost without the need for conscious thought. Right hand darting across to thumb open and enter the mouth of the Pete Ludwig bag, Alice quit Brad's side. She took two long strides across the hall, lowering her left knee to the floor on the third. Sinking into a kneeling position, she brought out her weapon. It was not a snub-nosed revolver such as most members of the B.W.O. carried, but a .45 calibre Colt Commander automatic pistol. Cupping her left hand under the right, she laid her sights on the centre of the Mexican's chest.

Swiftly though Alice moved, Brad had been even faster. Working in perfect harmony, his left hand drew open his jacket and made a clear access for the right to pass under and close about the combat grips of his big Government Model automatic. Pivoting the Colt from the grasp of the shoulder holster's spring clips, he adopted a combat crouch and turned the barrel into line on the man. In one sixth of a second, before the Cobra had cleared leather. Brad's pistol was positioned to drive a bullet into the other's chest if it should become necessary.

Still in the process of completing his draw, the Mexican found himself staring into a gun muzzle that looked much larger than its actual .45 of an inch. He noticed that the blond giant's thumb had pressed down the enlarged manual safety carch and his forefinger was resting on the trigger.

And that was no ordinary peace officer behind the big automatic. He was Deputy Sheriff Brad Counter, a *pistolero* of the first water; the man many claimed to be the most deadly gun-handling lawman in Texas.

Even before Alice had assumed her kneeling stance, the Mexican had reached a decision. Throwing aside his revolver the instant it left the holster, he shot his empty hands into the air.

'Don't shoot!' he screeched, remembering just in time to speak English. Then, deciding that some explanation of his behaviour was called for, he went on, 'Hey! You startled me, coming up like that.'

'I'd hate to give you a real fright,' Alice said dryly and stood up. 'Hit the wall. Assume the posture.'

Obediently, the man leaned with the palms of his hands flat against the wall. Although he was in a position which precluded the danger of his making any sudden movements, the deputies took no chances. Applying the safety catch, Brad returned the Colt to its holster. Then, making sure that he did not move into his partner's line of fire, he stepped behind the man. Quickly but thoroughly Brad patted over the other's body in search of more weapons. The blond felt a thick oblong outline in the man's inside breast pocket, but left investigating it until he had completed his work. Satisfied that the Mexican was no longer armed, Brad allowed him to straighten up but not to turn around. Drawing the man's arms behind his back, Brad clicked a pair of handcuffs on to his wrists.

'He's clean, Alice,' the big blond announced, taking a pace to the rear.

'All right, *hombre*,' the redhead snapped. 'What had you been doing in Della's apartment?'

'That I couldn't tell a lady,' the man replied. 'Seeing what she is.'

'Let's go and ask her what she is,' Alice suggested.

'Aw, why disturb her?' the man countered.

'I feel mean,' Alice answered. 'Knock on her door, Brad.'

'Look,' the Mexican said worriedly. 'I'll level with you. She's not at home right now.'

'Are you blacksmithing with her?' Brad demanded.

'Me!' yelped the man. 'I don't live off no hooker's earnings.'

'You came out of her apartment,' Alice pointed out. 'And you say she's not at home. Della wouldn't leave the door unlocked in a trap like this.'

'Maybe she sent him to collect her mail, Alice,' Brad remarked, reaching out to pluck a thick envelope from the man's inside pocket.

'That's mine!' the Mexican protested. 'The super loaned me his pass-key to get in.'

'Why, Della honey,' Brad drawled, looking from the name and address on the envelopc to the man. 'How you've changed.'

'Ain't you supposed to inform me of my rights under the Constitution?' the man asked sullenly.

Something about their captive's attitude puzzled Alice. instant reaction to the sight of herself and Brad had implied guilty knowledge. Yet he would have been unlikely to surrender so quickly, or peaceably, if he had suspected that they were coming to arrest him for Della Zekov's murder. His behaviour had been more that of a man confronted in, or just after, the commission of a less serious crime. Although he had acted instinctively, he had rapidly decided not to make his situation any worse by resisting arrest.

'You know, Brad,' the redhead remarked, putting her theory to the test. 'We should do just that, seeing that we're taking him in on a *twelve-fifty-six*.'

Surprise flickered across the man's swarthy features, like most criminals, he was fully conversant with the more common Articles of the Texas Penal Code. Caught red-handed as he had been, he could be charged under Article 1391 (Burglary of a private residence), which carried the penalty of a jail sentence not exceeding five years. Only that had not been the Article mentioned by Alice Fayde. She had said Article 1256 – and that was homicide; a capital felony punishable by imprisonment for life, or death.

'What's with the twelve-fifty-six bit?' the Mexican yelped. 'All I did was cop that letter. Look, take me back to her pad, you'll not find her stiff in it.'

Although heads had been peering out of doors along the hall, they disappeared with equal speed. People in that section of Evans Park might take interest in the activities of peace officers, but they did not intrude too closely on official business which did not directly concern them.

'Let's do that,' Brad ordered, glancing into the envelope. 'There's a fair wad of money in here, Alice.'

'Put it back in his pocket,' the redhead said, replacing the Commander. She took a man's handkerchief from her bag and used it to prevent her fingerprints getting on the Cobra as she gathered the weapon from the floor. 'Where's the key, *hombre*?'

'It's – I opened the lock with a piece of celluloid.'

'I figured you might have. Nobody has a lock that can be opened with a pass-key in a drum like this.'

'Shall we go in the hard way, Alice?' Brad inquired.

'No. We'll have it done legal. When did you see Della last, *hombre*?'

'Not in weeks,' the man replied. 'Look, I was in this bar just off The Street this morning and the bartender asked me to come round because Della hadn't showed in for work.'

'Since when did hookers start working this early in the day?' Alice asked.

'What do I know about hookers?'

'Your name's Sanchez and you've had more than one rap on 516.*'

'I didn't think you'd made me, Miss Fayde,' the man said ingratiatingly. 'Look, I'll level with you.'

'We were hoping you'd get around to it,' the redhead replied drily.

'I'm out of the rackets n—'

'Oh lord!' Alice ejaculated, sounding and looking exasperated. 'Take him in and book him with murder, Brad.'

'M–*Murder*!' Sanches croaked. 'Is Della dead?'

'You mean you *didn't* know?' Brad inquired with simulated surprise.

'Look, I was telling the truth some of the way,' the Mexican gabbled. 'Larry said that Mabel had took off last night without checking in and hadn't called this morning. So I should come over and see why not. When she didn't answer, I went in—'

'Through a locked door?' Alice challenged.

'So I broke in, is that against the law?'

'Surprising as it might seem to you, that's just what it is.'

'All right, already. So book me with a 1391. I went in and she wasn't there. Hadn't been back all night. I figured she must be off on a lay someplace and left—'

* Texas Penal Code Article 516, Offenses Against Morals Section (employing a prostitute).

'Don't tell me,' Brad put in. 'That envelope just jumped up into your pocket and you didn't have the heart to leave it all alone.'

'It was on the floor by the door, where the mailman had dropped it,' Sanchez corrected. 'When I saw what was in it, I figured I'd best take care of it for her.'

'It's too late in the year for snow,' Alice warned. 'How good's your eyesight, *hombre*?'

'Pretty good.'

'I'd say it's damned good, if you could see inside a sealed envelope.'

'All right, already!' the Mexican groaned. 'I picked it up, opened it and was going to cop the money. You want for me to put it in writing?'

'That's just what we want you to do,' the redhead confirmed. 'And, while you're at it, start thinking where you spent all last night from sundown on.'

'That's easy enough done,' Sanchez stated, not concealing his relief. 'I was shooting pool on McCullough until ten, then spent the rest of the night with a dame. I can give you her address.'

'Word has it that Della and Mabel Liebeck were fussing,' Alice remarked, escorting the man from the building after he had supplied the required information concerning his whereabouts the previous night.

'Sure,' Sanchez agreed. 'Larry had to split them out a few nights – Hey! Mabel called in yesterday that she wouldn't be around until Saturday.'

The problem of how to dispose of their prisoner and visit Mabel was solved for the deputies without effort on their part. Leaving the building, they found a G.C.P.D. radio patrol car parked behind their Oldsmobile. The crew had seen Unit S.O. 12 and waited in case their assistance might be required. Putting Sanchez into the patrolmen's charge and asking that he be held at the Evans Park Division's station house on a 1391 charge, Alice and Brad were free to continue with their investigation.

Reaching the apartment building in which Mabel lived, the deputies stood for a moment on the sidewalk. Looking at the first floor, the redhead pointed to one of the windows.

'That'll be Mabel's pad. The drapes are still closed, so she'll be at home.'

'I wonder why she's got that newspaper in the window?' Brad asked.

'We'll soon find out,' Alice guessed.

At the door of the hooker's apartment, the deputies drew their automatics. They did not know what kind of a reception awaited them and felt disinclined to take chances. If Della's extensive bruising had been anything to go by, Mabel might have had help to inflict it. That same help could be in the apartment with her and would respond in a hostile manner if the deputies knocked and announced their identities. On the way from Della's place, the partners had decided on their course of action.

Dropping his shoulder, Brad hurtled across the passage. Struck by the big blond's solidly built, two hundred and eighteen pound body, the door flew open. It's lock and chain bolt both burst under the impact, allowing Brad to erupt into the apartment. Following on his heels, but darting to his left side, Alice thrust up her Commander double-handed to make an arc with its muzzle around the room.

Screeching with fright, Mabel Liebeck sat up in her bed. Satisfied that the hooker was alone, Alice turned on the lights. Startled ejaculations broke from the deputies as they stared at Mabel. Snatching at the covers, the hooker jerked them up to conceal her naked torso. Before she could do so, Alice and Brad had observed that her body and face showed as many signs of injury as Della's corpse had displayed.

'Are you alone, Mabel?' Alice inquired, advancing while her partner closed the door.

'Looking like this,' the hooker answered bitterly, 'who'd be with me?'

'How did you get to look like that?' Alice asked, deciding that the injuries had not been inflicted the previous night.

'I fell down the stairs.'

'You and Della Zekov both?'

'Del – Hey! You mean those two kooks got to her—?'

'Which two kooks, Mabel?' Alice prompted as the hooker's words died away.

'Which two kooks would that be, Miss Fayde,' Mabel

countered. 'If I said anything, it must have been because I'm light-headed. Falling down—'

'Mabel!' Alice gritted. 'I didn't get any sleep last night and I'm worried sick over Joan Hilton being shot. So, for the lord's sake, don't play games—'

While his partner had been speaking to the hooker. Brad had drawn back the drapes. Leaving the newspaper where it had fallen, he walked towards the bed. In passing, he glanced at the dressing table. Three envelopes lay on it. They had been opened, but still retained their contents. Two held money and the other what looked like several photographs. There was something else on the table to attract his attention.

'Alice,' Brad put in, picking up the golden charm bracelet. 'Look here.'

'A guy gave it to me,' Mabel explained, seeing the interest displayed by the deputies.

'One of the charms is missing,' Alice pointed out.

'So I should say "no" because it's missing one charm?' Mabel demanded.

'Which two kooks, Mabel?' Brad changed the subject.

'I don't know what you're—' the hooker insisted.

'You came out of it better than Della,' Alice interrupted.

'So ask her—'

'We can't. She's dead.'

'D – Dead? You're putting me on!'

Having replaced the bracelet, Brad had extracted the photographs. The top one showed Mabel, wearing nothing but tattered tights and considerably marked up, draped across the shoulders of an almost naked woman, like an all-in wrestler caught in an airplane spin.

'She's dead, Mabel,' Alice repeated. 'Her neck was broken.'

'Maybe she landed badly when this gal here threw her for a picture,' Brad suggested, offering the photographs to his partner.

'You – You mean Hippolyta killed her?' Mabel croaked.

'Who did you say?' Alice demanded.

'Hippolyta,' the hooker replied. 'That's what that kook

"Mark" kept calling her. What the hell kind of name is that, anyways?'

'It could be the kind that will send her and this "Mark" hombre to jail for life,' Alice said grimly, holding the photographs in her left hand while she picked up the bracelet with her right and stared at the space left by the missing charm.

CHAPTER THIRTEEN

Alice Fayde saw the broken bottle just an instant too late to prevent it from puncturing the left front tyre of Joan Hilton's open-topped Ford convertible. In exculpation, for several seconds most of her attention had been directed to the light-coloured Pontiac hardtop car which had turned from a side street and was now following her.

If her suspicions should prove correct, Alice figured that she and Deputy Sheriff Jake Melnick – who was crouching on the floor behind her seat – might have to change the plans laid down to capture the killer of Emily Cochran and Amy Willer.

Having said so much, Mabel Liebeck had seen no point in holding back the rest of her story. So she had told of how she had met 'Mark', fallen for his story and accompanied him to meet the mythical rich businessman. She had described what had happened at the basement in pungent, vivid, but unladylike terms. While she had been unable to explain how she was returned to her apartment, she had mentioned 'Mark's' threat, the bonus she had received, and her reasons for not informing the police or the Syndicate of what had happened. She had been on the verge of changing her mind when the photographs had arrived through the mail and caused her to reconsider the consequences of doing so.

When it had come to describing her tormentors, Mabel had been less coherent. In fact, she had not presented the deputies with one item which could be construed as making the identification of the couple possible.

The best Mabel had been able to do about 'Mark' was to state that he had been below average height and not heavily built. Mousy brown hair, glasses, a pencil line moustache, brown suit of good quality, white shirt and dark bow-tie might be of some use, but not too much without more concrete details.

Mabel's comments on Hippolyta had been even more vague. Nor had the photographs offered any great assistance. On everyone of them, Hippolyta's face had been so distorted by excitement, elation, pain or the strain of supporting Mabel's weight, that it would be entirely different when in repose. Despite the apparent damage to Hippolyta's features, in the pictures where she was draped across the unconscious hooker, the deputies had known there was no help from that aspect. The remaining photographs had not shown Hippolyta bleeding, or badly marked, and Mabel had insisted that she was not responsible for the 'injuries'. So Alice and Brad had concluded, correctly, that make-up rather than blows had caused the woman's condition.

Pressed for further details, Mabel had described the Jeepster's custom fittings and given its licence number. She had declared that she had been unable to see outside the rear compartment. The only directions she could recollect had been the final right turn before mounting the sidewalk and dipping down to the garage's automatic doors.

Mabel had been taken to the Central Receiving Hospital so that her injuries could receive medical attention. On her return to the apartment, she had been accompanied by a policewoman who was to stay with her, posing as a friend on a visit, in case 'Mark' tried to make contact again.

The list of Glam-Batt's Texas-based customers and the report from the Houston Police Department had arrived in Thursday's mail. While the list had contained nothing immediately recognizable as a lead, the report had been more informative. For the first time, the Sheriff's Office personnel had become aware that there might have been a reason other than revenge for the attack on Joan Hilton.

In addition to listing the crimes committed by the unknown mugger, the report had stated that the final pair of victims were shot with a 9mm automatic pistol. However, the woman had been struck in the same manner as the previous victims before being shot and robbed. Comparing the photographs of the empty cartridge cases ejected in Houston with those found at the garage, the experts of the Firearms

Investigation Laboratory had detected sufficient similarities to assume that they had all passed through the same weapon.

Having remembered how the name 'Hippolyta' had figured several times in the correspondence columns of *Grapple*, Alice had made a telephone call to the New York Police Department. The magazine was produced in that city and she had asked if her New York colleagues could obtain the correct name and address of the person who used the queen of the Amazon's title. In the course of a recent case, Alice and Brad had obtained information which had helped the New York police to convict a notorious criminal.* So the girl knew that her request would receive prompt attention.

Although Mabel had intimated that her tormentors were wealthy, the gift of Amy Willer's bracelet and two rings which had belonged to Emily Cochran had given the motive for the crimes. 'Mark' was financing his movie-making in that fashion.

With the motive established, the problem of tracking down and arresting the killer still remained unsolved. Although the indications of wealth – 'Mark's' costly clothes, the converted Jeepster, the equipment in the basement – suggested an address in the high value part of the city, that still covered a fair-sized area. Nor, in an era of do-it-yourself addicts, could an electronically operated garage door be counted on as a certain indication of wealth. Unless some lead should make its appearance, the peace officers' best chance was to catch 'Mark' in the commission of a crime.

That chance had not come on Thursday, for no incidents concerning 'Mark' were reported. Joan Hilton was still unconscious and hovering perilously between life and death. The doctors fighting to save her could not even hazard a guess when, if at all, she would be capable of answering questions.

With regard to catching 'Mark', Sheriff Jack Tragg had been faced by a major problem of policy. He could give the whole story to the news media, warning the city's female residents of their danger; but if he did, he would cause the

* Told in *Point of Contact*.

killer to stop committing further crimes, at least for some months. Once the heat had died down, or in some other city, the man would most probably recommence his activities. That meant other women would suffer, or be killed.

So Jack had decided to put out decoys. Alice and other female officers would ride the streets of Lasher Division in open-topped convertibles and act as bait. In selecting the type of vehicles, the sheriff had demonstrated his ability to follow a criminal's line of thought. 'Mark' had not chosen any particlar style of car for his robberies in Houston. On his last job in that city, he had made a mistake in some way and been compelled to kill a male passenger he probably did not know about until too late. Despite the change in m.o., there had been sufficient evidence for the Houston police to accept the killings as being done by their unknown mugger. Clearly 'Mark' had learned from his mistake and now made sure that his victim was alone.

Being aware of the dangers, the sheriff had done everything possible to reduce them. Every woman officer would possess one qualification, at least a 'Marksman' rating with her handgun. Backing her up would be a male officer, crouching down or sitting on the floor behind the driver's seat. Added protection was to come from men, carrying assault armament, concealed in undercover vehicles at prearranged points over the area. If the decoy should catch 'Mark's' eye, she was to lure him past one of the stakeouts, find and turn into the driveway of a deserted house if possible, then halt. When Mark came to do his work, he would find himself trapped between two well-armed parties of peace officers.

Friday morning had brought an answer from New York. According to *Pussy-Grapple*'s records, 'Hippolyta' was the pen-name of a Miss A.P. Grindale. She had been a lieutenant in the W.A.C., based at Camp Logan, Missouri but was no longer in the service. Still a subscriber to the magazine, she had it mailed to a post office box number in Newark, New Jersey. The New York police had checked with the Newark office, to be told that Miss Grindale still maintained her box but had all the mail which came to it redirected to another box in Chicago.

Calling the postal authorities in Chicago, Alice had learned that Miss Grindale's box was still in use; but the mail which came to it was passed on to yet another box in Houston, Texas. Giving no thought to the Gusher City citizens whose taxes would pay the Sheriff's Office's telephone bill, Alice had next spoken to Houston. Unlike in the former cases, where Miss Grindale had rented the box and immediately turned in a forwarding address, she had collected her mail regularly until six weeks back. Then she had asked, once more, that it be redirected. This time to the main post office in Gusher City.

With something that definite to go on, Alice had contacted the Houston Police Department and asked if they could find out the names of any persons who had left that city in the past six weeks to take up employment in Rockabye County. Agreeing to try, the Houston officer had not been too hopeful. Nor would his department be able to spare men for the search until Monday, due to there being a Cattlemen's Convention taking place over the week-end.

Before going to check out the lead with the local post office, Alice had spent more of the tax payers' money by calling the provost marshal's office at Camp Logan, Missouri, and asking for all possible information on Lieutenant A. P. Grindale, W.A.C., who might have retired in the past eighteen months.

At the main post office, the deputies had located two counter clerks who recollected having handed over mail to a Miss Grindale. They had described her as a rather plain, but shapely, blonde woman in her early thirties, always stylishly dressed and wearing glasses with decorative frames. Not knowing that Hippolyta altered her wig and appearance when going to empty the box, Alice and Brad had felt that at last they had something to go on.

Nothing else had seemed to be paying off. According to the D.M.V., no Jeepster Commando station wagon bearing such a licence number was registered in Rockabye County. Nor had any of the local Jeepsters been fitted in the manner Mabel had described. I.C.R. had supplied the answer to the mystery number. It had been on one of a consignment of licence plates stolen from a Houston Steel Products' car-wrecking plant near Houston. The Jeepster's manufacturers had denied ever supplying a vehicle with such custom fittings. There were too many places where the work could be done to make checking up practical; even discounting the possibility of 'Mark' and Hippolyta having carried out the modifications themselves.

Arranging for 'Miss Grindale' to be detained when she next came to collect her mail, Alice and Brad had returned to the D.P.S. Building. They had joined in the preparations being made for the decoy duty.

As always, Jack Tragg had been determined to do everything possible to safeguard his officers' lives. Yet extreme precautionary measures would have been impossible, or likely to spoil the operation. If the way 'Mark' had organized his whole enterprise was anything to go on, he was intelligent enough to be wary of traps. That had been the reason why the sheriff could not allow an undercover vehicle to trail along behind each decoy convertible. So there would be stretches of streets, between the stake-out vehicles, along which the decoy must travel without supervision. If anything should go wrong, Jack Tragg had wanted to be sure that the officers in the open cars could protect themselves adequately.

At that point, the sheriff had been compelled, reluctantly, to decide that Alice and Brad could not work together as decoys. While the big blond could conceal himself in the back of Joan Hilton's convertible – borrowed by Alice as a gesture to her critically wounded friend – he could only do so by crouching in a cramped, uncomfortable position. Riding in such a posture would have stiffened his muscles to an unacceptable extent. Too much for Jack to permit him to take the risk. Yet Alice had charge of the case since the attack on Joan. She was also the best shot of all the female decoys.

There had been a simple solution to the problem. Deputies Grantly and Melnick had had to collect a prisoner from Tucson, Arizona. It had been easy to substitute Brad for the slender Melnick. Although Alice would have preferred to be working with Brad, she had realized that the sheriff was right on the issue and had raised no objections.

Friday night had passed uneventfully, with the decoys wending their ways through the streets of Lasher Division and ensuring that they had known the locations of the undercover vehicles. At half past eleven, Jack Tragg had called a halt to the operation for the night. Alice had returned to her apartment at the Chadwick Building and had caught up on some uninterrupted and much needed sleep.

With the sheriff's permission, Alice had turned in two hours late on Saturday morning. The answer from Camp Logan had been waiting on her team's desk. It had announced that 1st Lieutenant Annette Penelope Grindale had completed her hitch and left the service nineteen months back, but had not supplied a home address. She had enlisted in Los Angeles, stating that she was an orphan without surviving relatives. Most useful item in the report, although puzzling, had been her description. According to the army's records, she had had tawny-brown hair which was always kept cut short. Alice had not overlooked the possibility of a wig, or a bleach job to account for the post office clerk's statement that 'Miss Grindale' was a blonde. The woman's trade in the service had been physical training instructress; her hobbies and interests centred on her work, being gymnastics and unarmed combat.

Nothing further had developed on the case during Saturday. That night, there had been a flurry of excitement when Deputy Cuchilo and his driver, Sergeant Grace Emmett of the G.C.P.D.'s Airport Detail, had had a taker. Signalling with her wing lights to a stake-out vehicle in passing, Grace had carried out the rest of the plan and the sheriff's strategy had proved to be excellent. Boxed in between Grace's convertible and what had looked like a delivery truck, the taker could not have resisted with any hope of success. He had not wanted to resist, being a young man attracted by Grace's looks and hoping to get to know her better. After satisfying themselves that the taker could not have committed any of the crimes, he had been released with a warning not to accost strange women.

Sunday had been another quiet day, without the 'Mark' case, as it had become known, advancing any closer to a solution. Then, at eight thirty, Alice had picked up her tail.

Warning Melnick that they might have a taker, she had estimated the distance to the next stake-out. The answer had not been pleasing under the circumstances, for the under-cover car was at least half a mile away. They were on a winding residential street, with no convenient concealment points for the watchers. Nor could Alice do anything about alerting the waiting peace officers. A hand-held radio lay with her Colt Commander under a newspaper on the front passenger seat, but the tail was too close behind for her to use it undetected. She could only hope that nothing happened to scare off the taker before she had reached the stake-out.

'What the—?' Melnick hissed as the punctured tyre hissed out air and the Ford lurched.

'Blow out!' Alice replied without turning. She guided the convertible to the edge of the sidewalk and stopped. 'Keep down, Jake. He's going by!'

'No, he's stopping!'

'Not getting out, looking around!'

'He's opening the door!'

'Getting out and leaving it open!'

'Jake! I'm sure it's our man!'

'Get set to hit that radio,' Melnick replied. 'Is he close enough yet?'

'Nearly!' Alice breathed, barely moving her lips. 'The wily bastard. He's staying clear of my headlights. Take him, Jake. Now!'

'Peace officer here!' Melnick barked, lunging from his place of concealment behind Alice. 'Stand right where you are!'

Although the deputy held his revolver and had delivered the mandatory words of command, he wondered if they had caught the right man. Standing just beyond the glow of the convertible's headlights, gold-rimmed spectacles glinting like the windows of a diver's helmet, the small, insignificant figure looked about as harmless as a new-born baby.

And responded with the devastating speed of a striking sidewinder!

Moving as swiftly as either deputy had ever seen it done, the man went into the F.B.I. combat crouch. Flashing from behind his back, his right hand aimed a Luger automatic pistol by instinctive alignment. Twice flame spurted from the muzzle. Caught in the chest and head by the two 9mm bullets, Melnick pitched over the back rest of the seat and on to the rear of the car.

From the moment that the man had left the Pontiac, Alice had been studying him. As he had kept on the street and clear of the headlights, which she had planned to switch on in the hope of dazzling him, she could form only a general impression of his appearance. Not very tall, slender, wearing a dark suit, white shirt, bow-tie and fedora hat. Only the glasses fitted all the descriptions given by the various witnesses. She had automatically made a mental note of the Pontiac's number.

Could that small figure mincing daintily along really be the man who had shot and then pistol-whipped Joan Hilton?

That question had received a rapid answer in the affirmative.

Following Melnick's advice, Alice had reached cautiously with her right hand to feel under the newspaper and bring out the radio. For a moment Alice was paralysed with shock at the response to the male deputy's challenge. Then she dropped the radio and flopped to the right with her hand scrabbling away the paper to get at the Colt Commander. She had not moved a moment too soon. Turning from throwing lead into Melnick, the Luger cracked again. A hole blossomed in the windshield and Alice felt the wind of the bullet stir the hair on the side of her head. If she had reacted just a shade less quickly, she would have been hit.

Desperately Alice gripped the butt of the Commander. Jake Melnick had been hit badly, of that she felt certain. Stopping 'Mark' would be her responsibility and she knew that it would be anything but a safe, easy task.

Footsteps!

'Mark' was on the move!

Not towards the convertible, Alice realized, but running back to the Pontiac. Thumbing down the Commander's safety catch, Alice straightened her torso and rose. Already the small man had reached his car and was ducking in through the open door. Resting her elbows on the windshield, Alice supported her right hand with the left.

Why the hell hadn't she switched on the headlights? The interior of the Pontiac was a black mass through which she could not see to line her sights on 'Mark'.

Should she chance shooting blind at the position where the driver would be sitting?

With a crashing of gears, 'Mark' was preparing to get the vehicle into motion. There was only one certain way of preventing him from driving off. Fighting to stay cool, Alice altered her point of aim. Three times the Commander cracked, its cocking slide flashing backwards and forwards to eject the empty cases and replenish the chamber with the uppermost round in the seven-shot magazine. The first bullet whanged off the street's surface and into the air with a vicious-sounding whine. Although the second also ricocheted, it ended its flight in the bottom of the car.

Stay cool and keep aiming!

Alice's brain screamed the warning and her reflexes obeyed. For the third shot, she made an adjustment in the direction the Commander was pointing. Already the Pontiac was rolling forward. As the big automatic crashed, Alice's shooting instinct told her that she had made a hit. Sure enough, the car's left side rear tyre deflated explosively as the bullet tore through it.

Guiding the Pontiac to the left, 'Mark' brought it to a halt at an angle across the street. About to shoot again, Alice saw the long-barrelled Luger emerge from the open front window and heard the flat 'splat!' sound of its bullet passing her head. She had cause to be thankful for her partnership with Brad Counter at that moment.

Since the Colismides case, she and the blond giant had become very close. Some of Brad's almost fanatical interest in combat shooting had rubbed off and Alice had spent many off watch hours with him on the target ranges. During those periods, she had improved on the knowledge acquired compulsorily as a member of the B.W.O.

So Alice responded without needing to think. Dropping sideways to the left, she put the convertible's engine and dashboard between herself and 'Mark'. Three more bullets came, spiking an incline of holes through the windshield and following her down without striking flesh.

Silence followed, broken only by shouts of alarm which rose from the nearby houses. Cautiously Alice eased herself upwards. She knew that Melnick had been hit, but had no idea how serious his injuries might be. Maybe he could still be saved, if the threat of 'Mark' was removed. Gritting her teeth, Alice exposed herself and thrust the Commander in the direction of the Pontiac.

Clearly 'Mark' had not wasted time after causing her to take cover. The small man was haring on foot across a lawn towards the gap between two houses. With a mixture of relief and annoyance, Alice saw that both appeared to be unoccupied. Desperately she tried to draw a bead on the fleeing man, but his speed and the darkness combined to make him an elusive mark at which to aim. In a built up, residential area, she could not risk throwing bullets that might miss the man and fly on to the peril of innocent people.

Spitting out a furious comment, Alice opened the convertible's door and sprang on to the street. About to run after 'Mark', she changed her mind. Jake Melnick might need first aid. Better to let the little man go and hope that the net of official vehicles would find him than neglect a fellow officer and friend. Headlights glowed as the nearer stake-outs converged at all speed on the source of the shooting. People were approaching from the houses. Sick at heart, Alice went to the rear of the convertible. One glance told her all that she needed to know. That hole in the centre of Melnick's forehead meant he was beyond any human aid.

Turning slowly, the Commander dangling loosely at her side, Alice picked up the radio. She felt like breaking down and crying, but knew that she must get information on the air which, she hoped, would lead to 'Mark's' arrest.

CHAPTER FOURTEEN

HASTILY draping a negligee over her flimsiest nylon shortie nightie and matching briefs, Alice Fayde crossed her apartment's sitting-room. The door bell had just chimed and she was expecting to find Brad Counter outside. The time was eleven thirty and at that moment Alice hated everything to do with being a peace officer. After the events of the evening, she wanted somebody to treat her purely as a woman; to love her and to offer a shoulder upon which she could cry. She knew that Brad would fill that need.

Despite the tight net thrown around Lasher Division, 'Mark' had contrived to escape. At least, he appeared to have broken through the cordon, or hidden within its perimeter and was still at liberty. If he tried to flee from the city, he would not find things so easy. Operation Close Off had been put into being and – as had been demonstrated during the Tom Cord case – would effectively seal all exits from Rockabye County.

On hearing Alice's story, none of the other peace officers had blamed her for what had happened. Jack Tragg had stated that she had acted for the best all through what had been an unfortunate – although not entirely unforeseen – set of circumstances. In his orders, the sheriff had taken into consideration that all might not go as planned and desired. So he had commanded that, in the event of a decoy team being compelled to try and take 'Mark' without support, the female officer would handle the radio and call up reinforcements, allowing her male companion to concentrate on the arrest.

While her memory had still been fresh, Alice had tried to help a police artist to build up a composite picture of 'Mark'. To her extreme annoyance, she had found herself unable to produce one piece of information about the shape of his features. In fact, she could not even be sure of what kind of build 'Mark' possessed. Sensing the tension and frustration boiling inside her, First Deputy Alvarez had ordered her to log off watch and go home. After a good night's sleep, he had said, she would be able to think straighter.

What Ric Alvarez had not told Alice was how to get to sleep with all she had on her mind.

Shortly after she had reached home, the telephone had rung. Hoping that it would bring news of 'Mark's' arrest, she had been disappointed to hear the caller had dialled a wrong number. Hardly had she hung up when another call had come. It had been from Brad Counter. His flight had just landed and he had heard the news. Somehow the local radio and television stations had learned the details and had put out newscasts naming the peace officers involved in the shooting. The big blond had already contacted the D.P.S. Building and been told that Alice had logged off. He had promised that he would come over as soon as he had helped lodge the prisoner in the D.P.S. Building's cells.

Taking a quick shower, Alice had donned her most seductive night-wear. Never a promiscuous woman, she had been determined that for once she would let down the barriers and pull out all the stops.

The sound of the door bell had surprised her. Hardly enough time had elapsed for Brad to have concluded his duty, collected his M.G. MGB. convertible from the municipal employees' parking lot and reached the Chadwick Building. Of course, he might have arranged for his companion to deliver the prisoner and come over by cab from the airport.

Unlocking and opening the door, Alice suddenly realized – but just too late – that Brad had been with Ian Grantley; Jake Melnick's partner. With Grantley wanting to get finished so that he could go and help comfort Melnick's widow, Brad would have stuck with him to reduce the time spent on routine matters.

'Brad—!' Alice began, as the thoughts struck her.

'Hardly, Miss Fayde,' said the shorter of the two figures in the hall.

Usually Alice could both think and act with considerable

speed, especially in an emergency. The sight which met her eyes momentarily robbed her of the power to do either. Nor was her immobility caused entirely by the long barrelled Luger and Smith & Wesson Chief's Special snub-nosed revolver which pointed unwaveringly at her stomach.

Although she had seen him only as a vague shape beyond the illuminated area of the convertible's headlights, Alice identified the small, dapper, yet soberly dressed man. The Luger, his glasses and pencil line moustache furnished her with the necessary clues.

At 'Mark's' side stood a woman with mousey brown hair that Alice suspected was a wig. Although plain featured, Hippolyta – it must be her – could have turned male heads in any crowd. She wore a tight, sleeveless, low-cut black satin blouse which left her midriff bare, hipster toreador pants as tight as a second skin and high heeled, alligator hide shoes. The body covered by the garments was rich, full, voluptuous and sensual; if one discounted the firm ridges of muscle across the exposed, flat belly. She had a black cloak-coat hooked over her left arm and the right hand gripped the Smith & Wesson with casual competence.

Before Alice could think of resisting, the Burgenhofs moved forward. Retreating involuntarily, the redhead watched 'Mark' kick the door closed.

'You look surprised to see us, Miss Fayde,' Burgenhof remarked.

'Nope,' Alice replied, throwing a quick glance to where her Pete Ludwig bag lay on the sidepiece. 'You must be my new neighbours.'

'Do all your neighbours come in at gun-point?' Hippolyta inquired and her voice hardened. 'Forget the piece in your handbag. You'd never reach it.'

'What do I need with a piece?' Alice countered, hoping that she sounded a heap calmer than she felt. 'We figured you kooks would try a caper like this. The building's surrounded.'

'Is it now?' asked Burgenhof, not sounding too impressed.

'Would I lie to you?' drawled Alice. 'I only hope that they don't shoot you in here. I've just had the carpets cleaned.'

'Assuming, which my wife and I do not, that the building is surrounded, Burgenhof replied. 'Leave us not forget that *we* have *you.*'

'Before they got us, we'd see that you're too dead to care,' Hippolyta went on. 'Cover her, darling.'

'I'll do that,' Burgenhof promised, taking the revolver from his wife's hand without losing the drop on Alice.

Crossing to the sidepiece, Hippolyta opened the Pete Ludwig bag and returned carrying Alice's handcuffs. Although the small man looked incongruous holding the two guns, the redhead knew better than to try anything. He stood too far away for her to try jumping him and come out of it alive.

'Hands behind your back, Fayde!' ordered Hippolyta, approaching from behind the redhead's rear.

An eerie sensation bit at Alice as she obeyed. The situation was familiar, yet somehow strange. Then she realized why she felt that way. Not since her days at the Police Academy had she served in her present capacity. Since then, whenever handcuffs had been brought into use, it had been herself or her partner who operated them.

Give 'Mark' and Hippolyta their due though, Alice mused as Hippolyta dropped the cloak-coat and scientifically secured her wrists, they knew what they were doing. At no time did either of them present her with an opportunity of using her knowledge of self defence. Alice could not hold down a slight shudder as she felt the cold steel enfold and clamp on her wrists.

'All right,' the redhead said, holding her voice steady. 'So now we've played cops and robbers. What next?'

'Now we're going to play another game,' Hippolyta answered, retrieving the coat. 'It's called going for a ride to become a movie star.'

'We would have liked to do it here,' Burgenhof continued. 'But it is more convenient to take you with us.'

'Suppose I tell you to go to hell?' Alice inquired, guessing what the couple had in mind.

'I don't think you will,' the man stated. 'Because if you do, we won't hesitate to kill you immediately.'

'So let's get going,' Hippolyta commanded. 'Right now.'

'I don't mind if you don't,' Alice declared, glancing down over the nightie to the flip-flop slippers on her feet.

'Fortunately, we came prepared,' Burgenhof purred. 'Use your cloak, dear.'

Before Alice could object, Hippolyta had draped the cloak-coat over her shoulders. Reaching from behind, the woman fastened it in front of the redhead's throat. Large for its owner, the garment effectively concealed the scanty nature of Alice's attire.

'One thing, Miss Fayde,' the man warned, handing the revolver back to his wife. 'If we should meet anybody between here and our car, don't attempt to give an alarm.'

'If you do,' Hippolyta elaborated. 'We'll kill them as well as you.'

Nothing Alice had seen or knew about her captors led her to assume that they might be bluffing. As a peace officer, the redhead could not endanger the lives of innocent, chance-met people. What was more, she figured that the man and his wife were counting on that. Fortunately, the one person who could help her would not need any alarm raising to realize that something was wrong.

Causing no fuss, Alice allowed herself to be escorted from the apartment. They met nobody in the hall, riding down in the elevator, or while making for the side exit of the building. Alice was grateful for that. There had been a chance that any person they met would notice something was wrong and bring about his or her own death.

While crossing the well-lit parking lot to where a Plymouth four-door sedan was standing in the street, Alice looked in vain for her partner. Still 'Mark' and Hippolyta showed no sign of allowing her to turn the tables on them. The woman opened the rear door and ordered Alice to enter. While her husband took his place behind the steering wheel, Hippolyta followed the redhead in and sat nursing the revolver.

'Come on, Brad!' Alice thought. 'Where the hell are you?'

Apparently her partner was not within a distance at which he could receive thought-messages.

Alice possessed a thorough knowledge of Gusher City's

geography and she found no difficulty in deciding which way they were heading. Driving with his usual care, Burgenhof attracted no attention from the various police cars which were still prowling in search of him. Covered all the time by Hippolyta's revolver, Alice knew that any attempt to create a disturbance and alert one of the cars would result in her death. So she sat tight and waited for a better opportunity. From what her captors had said, that might present itself at their destination.

'Do you know why we came for you, Miss Fayde?' Burgenhof inquired as they left Lasher Division.

'To get even with me for running you off,' Alice replied and heard the man's annoyed exhalation of breath. 'You heard my name on the newscasts and found my address in the phone book. You called my number and when I answered, told me you'd hit a wrong number.'

'Correct, except for the first part,' Burgenhof admitted. 'You didn't scare me—'

'I know. You got turned about in the dark and thought you were charging at me instead of going away.'

'I'm looking forward to you,' Hippolyta hissed, while her husband showed his anger at the deputy's words.

'I left because I knew more cars would be on their way,' the man gritted. 'As you're the only person who might have been able to identify me, I decided to shut your mouth. Only it seemed such a waste to merely kill you. We've a better use for you.'

'To act as sparring partner for Hippolyta,' Alice guessed.

'How did you know my name?' the woman demanded, sounding startled.

'You'd be surprised just how much we-all know about you down to the Sheriff's Office,' Alice replied. 'It wasn't handed out to the news media, but we found Della Zekov's body the morning after you'd dumped it and Mabel Liebeck's told us all about your home movie business.'

'And now you'd like to know why we do it?' Burgenhof challenged.

'The police psychiatrist told us *that*,' the redhead assured him. 'Women have never taken you seriously and that hurt you. Watching them fight gives your ego a boost. You pretend they're fighting for you.'

'How about me?' Hippolyta said coldly, while Burgenhof shuffled uncomfortably at the deputy's knowledge of his motivation.

'Doctor Hertel had you pegged good,' Alice replied. 'He said you'd be a plain-looking woman. And that you'd had a real unlucky love affair, losing your man, or a succession of men, to glamorous girls. So you're taking your hate out on all women. He says, going by those breast-claw and the double knockout photographs, that you're a masoch—'

'Shut up, damn you!' Hippolyta snarled, jerking off the wig and flinging it down.

Anger boiled through the woman, for she knew just how close to the truth the psychiatrist's summation had been. Through high school and college, she had seen boy after boy in whom she was interested drift off with better favoured girls. It had been after she had lost the boy she had liked best to a campus beauty queen that she had developed her interest in fighting. In a movie theatre, watching the film *Yankee Pasha*, she had identified herself with Rhonda Fleming who had come off best in a fight with the glamorous 'harem girl', Mamie Van Doren. From then on, Hippolyta had become obsessed with the idea of fighting for her man. Although she had learned plenty about self defence, the opportunities to use it had been limited. In addition to seeking out films with girl-fight sequences, she had purchased home movies, photographs and cartoon-story booklets to support her yearnings for revenge. However, despite the various fantasies she had concocted for *Pussy-Grapple*, she had never managed to have a fight until her husband, and fellow devotee, had opened the way for her to do so.

'Darling,' Burgenhof remarked, cutting into his wife's thoughts as the car crossed the intersection leading to West Coolridge Avenue. 'I think there's a car following us.'

'Don't turn around!' Hippolyta snarled as Alice made a move to do so. Keeping the gun pressed against the redhead's side, the woman looked out of the rear window. 'Where?'

'It's a fair way behind,' the man replied. 'But I've been

seeing it on and off since just after we left the Chadwick Building.'

'Do you mean that imported heap coming up to the intersection?' Hippolyta demanded.

'That's the one,' Burgenhof confirmed.

'I've never seen a badge riding in one of them,' Hippolyta declared.

Alice felt a surge of elation. While the average peace officer's salary did not run to purchasing expensive foreign cars, Brad Counter drove a British convertible. Maybe it was her partner, who had somehow become aware of her predicament and was trailing along watching for his chance to rescue her.

'Oh well,' Burgenhof said, sounding relieved. 'He's not going to follow us now. He's tried to run a red light and a patrol car has stopped him.'

'Let's make the most of it, just in case,' Hippolyta advised.

Pressing his foot down on the accelerator, Burgenhof sent the Plymouth forward at a higher speed. Alice risked a quick glance to the rear, but already a corner hid the intersection from her sight. Racing along the winding street, Burgenhof guided the Plymouth around the right turn. He decelerated and, by deft use of the brakes, took them over the sidewalk to dip to the garage's door. Activated by the 'magic eyes's' beam, the door slid open and the car entered almost without stopping. Again Alice glanced behind. The door descended without her seeing the imported car go by.

Stopping the engine, Burgenhof climbed from the Plymouth. He crossed to the basement door and clicked on the garage's interior lights.

'Come on out!' Hippolyta ordered, after alighting.

With her hands manacled behind her back, Alice could not display any great agility while leaving the car. As she straightened up, Hippolyta unfastened and removed the cloak-coat. Tossing the garment into the car, the woman shoved Alice towards the door.

'So that's the Jeepster you use,' Alice remarked, nodding to the vehicle in question. 'Who fixed it up for you?'

'A man I knew in the Army,' Burgenhof replied, not relaxing his vigilance to any noticeable extent. 'It's most useful.'

'Not any more,' Alice warned. 'The sheriff's passed the word to all the hookers about your little game. The next time you proposition one, she'll yell copper so fast your head will swim.'

'We're not worried,' Hippolyta purred. 'We've found a new source of sparring partners. Get through that door.'

Allowing the women to precede him, Burgenhof switched off the garage's lights and closed the door. Alice heard the click of the Yale lock she had noticed in passing. She had also seen what a solid structure the door was. Breaking it open would be a task beyond even her blond giant of a partner.

Steering Alice to the table by the wrestling mat, Hippolyta told her to spread apart her feet, bend forward and rest her head against the wall. Knowing that the time for resistance had not yet come, the redhead obeyed. Everything had been made ready, she had noticed; cameras set up, lights positioned, even the equipment supplied for patching up the fighters between rounds. She felt her wrists freed and the boxing gloves slipped into place on her hands. Not until the tapes had been tied was she permitted to straighten up. Before she could turn, two hands grasped and tugged at her nightie's shoulder straps. The material ripped and the garment slid downwards.

'Let it go!' commanded Burgenhof from just behind her. The cold muzzle of a gun emphasized his words and prevented Alice from trying to hitch up the nightie. 'Turn around.'

Hands going involuntarily to cover her naked bust, Alice obeyed. Burgenhof had stepped away after tearing the straps. His Luger was on the table and he held the Smith & Wesson. Standing at the table, Hippolyta had no use for the gun right then. She had already removed her shoes and blouse. Reaching behind her, she unclipped and slid off her bra.

'My wife doesn't want any unfair advantage, Miss Fayde,' Burgenhof announced, backing off to join Hippolyta. 'Please don't try to escape while I'm lacing on her gloves.'

Watching the little man thrust the revolver into his waistband, prior to fastening the tapes of the gloves his wife had drawn on, Alice worked her arms to clear the stiffness from them. There was only one way out for her; a slender one at that. She must go along with her captors' wishes. Given luck, once 'Mark' was concentrating on his camera, she could knock Hippolyta cold and jump him before he realized the danger. Only, studying Hippolyta's muscle development, Alice knew that carrying out her plan would be anything but a sinecure.

'On the mat, please, Miss Fayde,' Burgenhof said, almost as politely as if making a request that could be refused.

Flipping off the slippers, which would have been more an impediment than an aid, Alice obeyed. Her hands had fluttered up to her bosom at the words and she stood like that as Hippolyta approached her. The woman shaped up like a professional boxer, Alice noticed. There was no fooling about Hippolyta, she knew what she was doing.

Studying Alice, Hippolyta felt vaguely disappointed. The woman had hoped that the deputy would display some ability instead of standing in that embarrassed, defenceless manner. Maybe she would show better in the next session. In which case, Hippolyta decided to make the most of her chances. She knew just how much of an advantage she had previously gained by the boxing interludes and figured that this was one time when she might need it.

Out jabbed Hippolyta's left, aimed towards Alice's unprotected nose. Instantly the redhead turned from passive to active. Blocking the blow, she drove a left hook into her assailant's belly. Grunting a little. Hippolyta rocked on her heels. Three fast, short jabs to the woman's bust kept her off balance. Her guard dropped to shield the attacked area. Across flashed Alice's right, catching the side of Hippolyta's jaw. Spinning around, the woman hit the mat on her hands and knees. Even as Alice prepared to follow up her advantage, Burgenhof stepped clear of the still-rolling camera and snatched the revolver from his waistband.

CHAPTER FIFTEEN

A TRAFFIC light glowed redly, causing Brad Counter to bring his M.G. MGB. convertible to a halt. While waiting for it to change, he looked along the street and had a clear view of the Chadwick Building's parking lot. At first he watched the three people about to board a Plymouth four-door sedan with little more than casual interest. One of the women wore clothes which showed that she possessed a better than average body. However, in Brad's considered opinion, and seen from a distance of something over two hundred and fifty yards, her shape was no better than his partner's.

Hell's fire! The second woman *was* his partner.

Now why would Alice be going out at this late hour? She had known that Brad was on his way and, going by the way her voice had sounded over the telephone, had been wanting him to arrive. What was more, where had the cloak-coat she was wearing come from? Brad knew that she did not have such a garment in her wardrobe.

Something was very wrong!

Then Brad knew what it was, or – unlikely and improbable as it sounded – might well be.

The man who had taken the Plymouth's driving seat had been of less than medium height, slender in build, dapper and wore glasses. At that distance Brad could not make out whether he had a pencil-line moustache. Although the woman did not have blonde hair or glasses, she sure as hell possessed a good figure.

It could not be 'Mark' and Hippolyta!

Or could it?

Only a psycho would be out on the streets, knowing that he had almost certainly been seen by a peace officer trained to remember and describe physical features. Of course,

Doctor Hertel had cast doubts about 'Mark's' sanity. Certainly his motives for robbing and killing had not been those a rational, mentally-stable human being. Through all his activities, however, had run traces of careful thought and planning to avoid detection.

Alice had been the peace officer who had seen and might be able to describe the man who called himself 'Mark'.

Even as Brad's left hand dropped to the M.G.'s brake and he prepared to send the little car leaping to intercept the Plymouth, something inside his head rang a warning. It had been his intention to charge to the rescue, force the other vehicle to halt and spring from his car with the big Colt automatic in his hand. Cold, hard logic took control of him before he could commit such a dangerous piece of folly. Following his first inclination could get his partner killed.

Alice had not accompanied the man and woman of her own free will. There must be a gun in her ribs, literally and most probably figuratively, to make her comply with the couple's demands.

So what was the best thing to do?

Again cold logic gave the answer. Follow the other car to its destination. Once there, Alice's captors were less likely to be expecting trouble and would be just that little bit easier to deal with. There was only one, but very great, danger: he would lose sight of the Plymouth. Luckily, he had done a fair amount of training in tailing with a motor vehicle and believed he could put his knowledge to good use. There was not too much traffic on the streets at that hour, which was both help and hindrance. It meant that he would be better able to keep the Plymouth under observation, but also that he could not go too close in case he aroused the suspicions of Alice's captors.

Starting the M.G., Brad made no attempt to close the distance with the other vehicle. Nor did he signal to attract the attention of the patrol cars which occasionally went by. While any one of them could have supplied him with the means to contact Central Control and pass the word of Alice's predicament, he would have to halt first. In doing so, the delay could cause him to lose the Plymouth.

On the two cars rolled, until the leader passed across an intersection on a permissive green light. Ahead lay a winding street of what was the kind of area in which a man like 'Mark' might possibly have his home. The houses would be owned by members of the upper middle-income bracket and the deputies had suspected that their man came into that category.

Just as Brad drew near, the traffic lights flickered through to red. If he obeyed their instructions, the Plymouth might give him the slip. So he kept the M.G. moving. Looking to the left as he passed over the intersection, his gaze met with a sight that did not please him.

As the old saying went, 'There's never a cop around when you need one.'

Alternatively, when one could quite happily do without meeting the forces of law and order, its members could be counted on to make an appearance.

Brad utter a silent prayer that the crew of the r.p. car would be old hands. If so, all might be well. Experienced officers of long service tended to overlook harmless traffic violations; which meant spending off watch hours in court if taken up.

Either the car was manned by young patrolmen, eager to keep up their quota of pinches, or its crew were feeling conscientious. Whatever the reason, the r.p. lunged from its position and followed the M.G. There was only one thing to do. Although Brad believed that his souped-up convertible could outrun the r.p., doing so would offer him no solution. The car's crew would give chase 'Code Three' and its wailing siren was going to attract the people in the Plymouth's notice. So Brad pulled over to the curb, stopped the M.G. and reached into his jacket.

Halting to the rear of Brad's convertible, the r.p.'s crew did not appear to be in any great hurry to continue with their duty. When they moved, it was in a significant manner Both front doors opened, to let the driver and shotgun emerge. While the former stayed on the street, his partner advanced parallel with him along the sidewalk. Their hands hung just a touch too negligently close to the butts of their holstered revolvers. That was the behaviour of peace officers approaching a suspect, rather than patrolmen coming to serve a citation for a traffic violation.

Of course, the caution was understandable under the circumstances. A dangerous criminal had evaded arrest that night, he was alone and believed to be using a car of some kind. Any peace officers approaching a vehicle with a solitary male occupant would be disinclined to take chances. If Brad had had the top of his M.G. open, the r.p.'s crew might have recognized him. He did not and was paying for the lapse by being delayed.

When close enough to make out the blond giant's bulk, the officers relaxed their vigilance a trifle.

'All right, mister,' the shotgun drawled, bending to look inside the M.G. 'We don't like commies either, but that red light's not in honour of Ho Chi—'

'The name's Counter, I'm a deputy sheriff,' Brad interrupted, showing his identification wallet with its photograph and badge of office. 'Hit your radio, *pronto*. Tell Cen-Con to notify all units in this area to look out for a dark-coloured four door Plymouth sedan, no license number, driven by a small man and with two women in the back. Proceeding along—?'

'West Coolridge Avenue, Leander – sir,' the shot gun supplied as Brad's words ended in an interrogation mark.

The use of the final honorific had come as a diplomatic afterthought. A deputy sheriff held equivalent rank and disciplinary powers to a Patrol Bureau's lieutenant. As such, that big blond could stir up a whole heap of trouble for a couple of patrolmen who – even inadvertently and with good cause – had inconvenienced him by their behaviour.

'Tell them to observe, report, but not to intercept,' Brad went on. 'The suspects are holding Woman Deputy Fayde hostage in the car.'

'Hell's fire!' ejaculated the shotgun, turning to sprint back to the r.p.

The final words had put the affair in a different complexion. Any deputy requesting assistance could expect to be given it; but never more so than when another peace officer was in trouble.

'Can we help, sir?' the driver asked.

Yes or no for the answer?

Brad thought fast. Already the Plymouth had passed out of his sight. Of course, he could maybe catch up with it. Balancing the danger of the r.p. being noticed by Alice's abductors against its value as a means of communication and information, the big blond opted for the latter. Having support readily available might spell the difference between life and death for Alice.

'Follow me,' Brad ordered. 'But kill your red light and keep directly to my rear.'

'Yo!' confirmed the driver, understanding the reason for the last instruction. Even without the flashing red light on top, the colour of the r.p. was selected to make it conspicuous. By keeping the M.G. between them and the Plymouth, they would be less noticeable.

'Give me one flash with your side lights when Cen-Con acknowledges,' Brad continued, before the patrolman could follow his companion. 'Two as soon as any report comes in.'

'Yo!' the driver repeated and, seeing that Brad was making ready to set off, ran to the r.p. car.

Letting the M.G. build up its speed, Brad drove along the winding, hilly street. Behind him, the r.p. car was following his orders to the letter. A flash of the side lights informed the big blond that Central Control had relayed his message to all official vehicles in that area.

Satisfied, Brad concentrated on the road ahead, alternately darting glances at the buildings on either side. His gaze took in the fact that a street climbed up each ridge close to where West Coolridge Avenue entered a high-walled draw. Going through the draw, he made the sharp right turn and followed the curve back to the left. He was now on what appeared to be plain Coolridge Avenue, without the compass-point addition to its title. Still no sign of the Plymouth, but the road wound too much for extensive visibility. Almost three quarters of a mile beyond the eastern end of the draw, he saw a red light flashing and a black Detective Bureau car cruised from the opposite direction to which he was going. At Brad's signal, the car came to a halt. The big blond and his escort drew up facing it.

'Have you seen the Plymouth?' Brad called, through the M.G.'s open window.

'Nope,' the detective driving the other vehicle replied. 'We've been down by the interesection back there for maybe twenty minutes and it hasn't gone by.'

Leaving their vehicles, the peace officers gathered at the M.G. All could see the strain on the blond giant's face and waited to hear what he planned to do next. Brad looked in the direction from which they had come. There had been a couple of streets turning off Coolridge Avenue on this side of the draw and the other two beyond it.

'Do you know of any houses near here with automatic garage doors?' the big deputy inquired.

'There may be some,' replied the senior detective. 'But I've never heard tell of them.'

'You boys make a sweep to the left,' Brad instructed the r.p.'s crew after the others had failed to supply him with the required information. He nodded to the detectives. 'And I'd be obliged if you'd take the right. If you've got a hand-held radio, I'd admire to borrow it.'

'I'll fetch mine from the car,' promised the second detective and did so.

Placing the radio on the passenger's seat of the M.G., Brad watched the other men set off to their appointed areas. Making a U-turn, the big blond drove back towards the draw. He went through and selected the left hand side street. Climbing up, he saw a r.p. car ahead and flagged it down.

'Nothing's come this way,' declared the shotgun. 'We've been along here checking out a prowler report and would've seen it.'

'We'd even have seen it if it'd gone up the other side,' the driver went on. 'Since your call came through, we've been watching both here and there.'

'Why'd they grab Miss Fayde off?' the shotgun inquired.

'I'm damned if I know,' Brad admitted. 'Maybe they hope to trade her for a free run across the border.'

While retracing his course down the slope and turning east through the draw, Brad pondered on the patrolman's question. Deep at the back of his memory, a thought fought to come through. It was something he could not bring back to full being, but which he instinctively knew must be important and of bearing to the situation.

Why had the couple kidnapped Alice?

Certainly not to be used as a bargaining point in winning uninterrupted passage into Mexico. The authorities below the border would be only too willing to arrest and hold them for extradition.

To remove the only person who had been granted a long, frontal look at 'Mark' and lived?

If so, why had they not done it in her apartment?

There was one other possibility came to mind. What if that pair of nuts had taken the incredible risks so that they could make another movie, using Alice as they had Della Zekov and Mabel Lieb—

That was it!

Memory had come flooding back at his recollection of Mabel's name. It was helped by the fact that he was already turning around the end of the draw. The hooker had been able to recall only one detail of her journey in the Jeepster. Just before it had ended, the vehicle made a sharp right turn, bumped up and across a sidewalk, then dipped down to the doors of the garage.

Reaching the garage of the house he was just passing would call for all those manoeuvres.

Brad stopped his car and stepped from it. Yes, that house could supply all the features required for Mabel's destination. Or it might be no more than a coincidence that they fit. There was only one way to find out. The house showed no lights, nor signs of life. That could mean its owners were in bed, or down in the sound-proof basement indulging in their bizarre pastime.

Reaching through to take a small flashlight from the M.G.'s glove compartment, Brad looked at the borrowed radio. After a moment, he decided against summoning assistance. If he was wrong, one peace officer was sufficient to be involved. Should he be right, more men would mean an increase in the possibility of detection. If 'Mark' and Hippolyta found out that their secret had been discovered, Alice might count her life expectancy in seconds.

Stepping silently, Brad descended the inclined driveway and halted before the garage. At the bottom edge of the door were two stout metal handles in case the owner should wish to open it manually. Brad listened at the door and tried to find the means to look inside. None presented themselves, so he decided that there was only one thing left to do.

Go in and make his examination at close range.

Setting his feet slightly apart, Brad bent and took a firm hold of the handles. Then he started to strain upwards with all the strength in his giant frame. At first nothing happened, except that perspiration poured down his face and the back of his jacket expanded until it was in danger of being burst open by the writhing muscles underneath. Dragging air in through his nostrils and clenched teeth, Brad threw all he had into his efforts.

Just as he thought that he had failed, the blond deputy heard a faint, sharp crack. The catch of the lock had snapped under the strain and the door opened swiftly. Unable to halt his exertions, Brad watched the door rising far faster than he had intended. Yet it moved in silence, thanks to Burgenhof having kept its pivots, guides and mechanism well-lubricated to facilitate a speedy entry to the garage.

No lights showed from inside the garage and, more important, nobody declared resentment of Brad's actions by throwing lead at him. Drawing his Colt, he stepped cautiously into the building. Instantly all his doubts ended. The flashlight he had produced and lit with his left hand illuminated a dark blue Plymouth four door sedan. Next to it was a Jeepster Commando station wagon, only it was no ordinary production line machine. Black in colour, its rear section had no windows. That was the mysterious vehicle which had carried the two hookers to meet the nonexistent rich businessman.

From the vehicles, Brad swung his light around the garage. Crossing to the door, he tried to listen to what was going on beyond it. No sound pierced it and he could see from its sturdy construction that he could neither kick nor charge it open.

CHAPTER SIXTEEN

SEEING Burgenhof lining the revolver at her, Alice wondered if he meant to shoot in order to protect his wife.

'Stand still, Miss Fayde,' the little man ordered. 'Attacking an opponent when she's down is against the rules.'

Despite the mild voice, Alice knew better than to disobey. So she made no attempt to carry out her original plan. Instead, she stood with the gloved hands dangling loosely at her sides and watched Hippolyta. On her hands and knees, the woman shook her head from side to side to clear it. Then she forced herself upwards. Anger flashed on the plain features as Hippolyta glared at the redhead. As soon as his wife had regained her feet, Burgenhof crouched behind the camera and sighted it. He operated the mechanism with his left hand, retaining the Smith & Wesson in his right. Clearly he did not intend to chance being caught by surprise.

For a few seconds, Alice and Hippolyta eyed each other's faces. The woman watched for signs of fear, hesitancy or uncertainty, but found only a cold, grim alertness that differed from anything she had seen displayed by a hooker. For her part, the redhead's scrutiny was searching for a hint of how her assailant meant to attack.

Most of the odds were on Hippolyta's side and Alice did not delude herself on that score. The woman had a slight height and weight advantage and would probably be somewhat stronger. Experience would be on her side, too. Although the Bureau of Women Officers gave its members a thorough grounding in self defence and unarmed combat, its curriculum did not include formal boxing. The female officers were taught to block and throw the various punches; but their training stressed judo throws and locks, or the dirtier aspects of quickly subduing an attacker, rather than straight fist fighting. From the way Hippolyta handled herself, she had learned her boxing lessons very well. On top of that, she had a definite mental edge due to her masochistic delight in accepting punishment; and out of the fact that the redhead was aware of it.

'Fight on!' Burgenhof called, a hint of impatience in his voice.

With a quick, two-footed shuffle, bare feet slapping on the mat and bosom bouncing in tune to the sharp, springy steps, Hippolyta attacked. She bored in low, throwing a long, raking left at Alice's stomach. The redhead tried to cover up, failed and took a heavy dig just over the top of her briefs. Grunting a little, for the blow had hurt, Alice flung her right fist at the woman's face. The glove thudded sharply against Hippolyta's left eye and her sudden intake of breath told Alice that the blow had hurt. Not that the woman retreated. She stood her ground and thrust a right jab into Alice's midriff. Muscles tensed and braced, the redhead took the blow with no great sign of distress. A sharp exchange of punches developed. Each protagonist scored several times on the other's head or body before they broke away to catch their breath.

Circling each other warily, Alice and Hippolyta studied and made a mental appraisal of what had happened to that point.

For the first time, the deputy became aware that Hippolyta had not come unscathed through her meetings with the two hookers. Although make-up had concealed it, Alice's blows to the face had exposed the discoloured area around the woman's left eye. An almost flesh-tinted patch of sticking plaster was affixed to the side of Hippolyta's right breast. She must have been fortunate to have come through encounters with two tough girls like Mabel and Della and to have suffered no greater injuries. Of course, her insistence on boxing as an opening sequence would have given Hippolyta a decided advantage.

For her part, the woman noticed the reddening caused by her gloves impacting on Alice's body. No serious damage appeared to have been done to the deputy and she gave no hint of fear or trying to break off the fight.

Keeping his camera focused and running, Burgenhof breathed heavily. He wished that the women would start mixing it again. Sweat flowed freely down his face and soaked through his shirt. Wriggling in exasperation at the delay, he opened his mouth ready to order the women to continue.

As if she had read her husband's thoughts, Hippolyta moved in. Alice met her with a flurry of rapid, stabbing blows at the head. Scoring often enough to make the swelling on Hippolyta's cheek increase, she also destroyed the woman's co-ordination for a moment. Hippolyta missed with a left hook, took a right jab to the bust and countered with a left uppercut to Alice's belly. Ignoring the hurt caused by the blow, Alice slammed her right glove on to the blue-black patch on the woman's face. A swift bound rearwards carried Hippolyta out of range of further punishment. She half turned as if badly hurt and pivoted back as Alice came after her. The redhead saw her danger too late. Out thrust Hippolyta's right in a punch which ended in the centre of the deputy's face. Stopped in her tracks, Alice snorted at the blood which suddenly clogged her nostrils.

Another brisk, savage mill commenced, continuing for several seconds. When the women separated, they had both taken hard knocks. Breathing heavily, with sweat spread in a glossy sheen over their naked torsos, they stood watching for a resumption of hostilities. The blood from Alice's nose ran in a steady flow, splashing down on to her body. Gore smeared Hippolyta's chin and throat from a laceration on her lower lip. From the raw-looking, inflamed patches on her ribs and stomach, she was having her passion for receiving pain gratified.

Rubbing at her swollen eye, Hippolyta frowned. Alice was proving to be a tougher proposition than any of the hookers had been. While their efforts had been unskilled and wild, the redhead was fighting scientifically. When she scored, every time and not on occasion as luck favoured, her blows hurt. Maybe enough to swing the fight in her favour.

How would Oscar react if he saw his Hippolyta, of whom he had always been so proud, go down in defeat?

Stirred by that thought, Hippolyta rushed at Alice. However, the woman went with a definite plan in mind. Pretending to guard her injured cheek, she left her body open in a most tempting manner. Just as she had expected, the redhead took the bait. Crouching slightly to put more weight behind her arm, Alice slammed home a wicked left hook flush into the hemisphere of Hippolyta's right breast. In doing so, she had set herself up perfectly for Hippolyta's right hook to the side of her head.

Before Alice's blow ripped home, Hippolyta cut loose with her planned reprisal. Simultaneous noises rose, the slapping thud of the body punch and the harder, sharper crack of the hook. Hippolyta fell back, gasping in pain and blinded by the tears it caused. Desperately she sought to bring her whirling senses under control, fighting down an urge to clasp the stricken area with her hands so as to keep her guard up. Then her vision cleared and she discovered why the redhead had not followed up the advantage. Alice had been spun around by the force of the hook and had fallen to the floor. However, she was already kneeling up, sucking in deep breaths and shaking her head. The blow had dazed her, but its effects were wearing off. A livid mark showed where the punch had landed, partly on her left cheek and partly on the eye and the swelling was already visible.

Stopping the camera as Alice remained on the floor, Burgenhof stepped to the table. He laid down the revolver, removing his jacket and bow-tie then opening the neck of his shirt. Retrieving the weapon, he returned to the camera.

'Excellent, so far, my dear,' the man enthused, breathing almost as heavily as either of the women. 'And you, Miss Fayde. But surely you haven't given up already?'

Slowly Alice began to rise. With something like elation, she saw an expression of consternation and just a hint of fright creep across Hippolyta's face. Then the woman rushed at her, without allowing her the opportunity to stand all the way up. With the other's gloves lashing at her, Alice was driven backwards across the mat towards the wall.

* * *

In the garage, Brad Counter reluctantly conceded that he could do nothing to enter the basement. Not from his present location, at any rate. Given the right equipment and without the need to care how much noise was made, the door could be broken down. If it was attempted under the prevailing conditions, by the time on entry was effected Alice would be dead.

Swinging on his heel, Brad strode from the garage. He was about to look for another means of ingress when he realized what he must do first. If anything should go wrong, he had no wish to permit 'Mark' and Hippolyta to escape. So he walked back to the M.G. and lifted out the General Electric two-way, hand-held Voice Commander radio.

'Deputy Counter to Cen-Con!' the big blond said into the speaker.

'Cen-Con by,' answered a voice Brad recognized as belonging to a svelte, somewhat snooty civilian dispatcher.

'Have located residence owned by "Mark" and Hippolyta,' Brad announced and could imagine the hush that his words would bring down at Central Control. 'It's Number One, Coolridge Avenue. Repeat, *Coolridge* Avenue, not—'

'Message Understood, Deputy Counter,' the dispatcher interrupted coldly. 'I live on *West* Coolridge and know the diff—.'

'Get me some help here, honey-child,' Brad requested. 'Tell them to come "Code Two"* and surround the house. I'm going in—'

'Wait for assistance to arrive, Deputy—'

'Like hell, honey-child. They've got my gi— partner in there—'

'Departmental rules . . .!' the dispatcher cut in frigidly.

'Tell them to surround the place,' Brad repeated. 'If Alice and I aren't out in fifteen minutes, we won't be coming.'

Giving the dispatcher – who he could imagine was turning red and preparing to repeat her warning of the Department's rulings on such situations – no chance to speak, Brad switched off and returned the radio to the car. He knew that neither Jack Tragg nor Chief of Police Phineas Hagen approved of their officers 'cowboying', going into dangerous situations alone when help could be obtained; but he figured that he was justified under the circumstances. If he had

* Code Two: radio code for emergency, but do not use red light or siren.

guessed correctly about the reason for Alice's kidnapping, she might be taking a hell of a beating at the hands of her captors.

Passing along the side of the garage, Brad reached the rear of the property. He was fully aware of one danger. Obviously none of 'Mark's' and Hippolyta's neighbours knew of their bizarre hobby, so the deputy ran the risk of his purpose being misunderstood. If he should be seen by the people in the next house, they might take him for a prowler. Provided that they restricted their attentions to calling the police, it would not be so bad; but they could decide to take a more personal interest. Brad had no desire to waste time in explanations, nor to be shot by an outraged householder who believed that he was doing a good turn for a neighbour.

All the blond giant's anxieties on that score ended as soon as he reached the rear of the building. Hippolyta had frequently sun-bathed in the nude and, in the interests of privacy, the Burgenhofs had had a fence erected which hid the garden from the neighbours' view.

More in hope than expectation, the deputy tried the back door. It was locked, and bolted at top and bottom. Going to the kitchen window, he peered through at the dark interior. Pivoting free his Colt automatic, he sucked in a breath and muttered a silent prayer. Tapping the upper pane of glass sharply, Brad wondered if he had ever heard such a crack and clatter as it made in breaking.

Silence fell after the broken glass had spattered to the kitchen's floor. No voice raised in alarm. No lights flickering on as 'Mark' or his wife came to investigate. Reaching in, Brad unfastened the catch and raised the lower half of the window. Five seconds later, he stood inside the house. Holding the flashlight out at shoulder height and arm's length in his left hand, to confuse anybody who saw it and figured on shooting him, he crossed the room. In the hall, he swung the beam as he searched for the way to reach the cellar. That door under the stairs struck him as being a good bet.

Putting to use all the ability he had gained when hunting whitetail deer, or stalking trout along a heavily-fished river, Brad moved silently towards the door. It opened at his push and he began to descend the flight of stairs. Alert for any hint of danger, he wondered why the sound of the window being broken had not brought 'Mark' to investigate. Then he saw the reason. If Burgenhof had spoken the truth to Mabel, the basement was sound proof. Which meant its walls kept sound *out* as well as in.

At the foot of the stairs was a door. It had a Yale lock which would most likely be fastened. If it should be as stout as the entrance from the garage, the blond giant realized that he would still be unable to reach his partner.

* * *

With blows seeming to be coming at her from every angle, Alice retreated across the mat. She covered up as well as she could, bending her torso forward and raising her arms before it while the gloves partially shielded her face and head. Instinctively she permitted her assailant to expend energy and wind in the onslaught. As she reached the wall, Alice could sense that Hippolyta's attack was flagging. Coming out of her crouch, she hurled a right cross which threatened to flatten the woman's right breast. A croaking squeal burst from Hippolyta's lips. She tottered away from the redhead with blood oozing through the piece of sticking plaster on the wound.

Raw agony blazed through Hippolyta and it was not of a kind in which she could feel her masochistic pleasure. When Alice came after her, she clinched desperately. Clinging to the redhead's waist, the women only partly succeeded in her intentions. She had ensnared the deputy's left arm, but the right remained actively at liberty. Locked together as tightly as a pair of lovers, Alice and Hippolyta staggered in a half-circle and towards the centre of the mat. The redhead hooked repeatedly with her free fist into Hippolyta's ribs and at the side of the tawny head.

Moaning in tune with the blows which continued to land on her, Hippolyta jerked up her right knee. Passing between Alice's legs, it struck the base of the briefs. Although their proximity had prevented the impact attaining its full force, the redhead cried out in pain. Clamping her thighs together to prevent a repetition of the attack, Alice tiled back her head. Before Hippolyta saw the danger, Alice butted her viciously. The unyielding bone of Alice's forehead cracked on to Hippolyta's nose. Letting out a shriek, the woman released her hold. Blood flooded from her nostrils as she tottered away, hands flying to her face.

Sobbing for breath, with exhaustion and nausea threatening to overwhelm her, Alice exerted every bit of will power to remain on her feet. She was fighting for her life and knew it. Clearly Brad had been unable to deal with the r.p. car's crew swiftly enough to catch up and learn where she was being taken – assuming, of course, that the imported vehicle had been driven by her partner. In which case, she was on her own. In her present physical condition, she would not have the speed or strength to tackle 'Mark'. So she would be killed as soon as the fight ended; or after Hippolyta had recovered sufficiently to work Alice over some more. The woman would not accept anything less than death after what had happened. Alice decided that, if she was going to be killed for the pair of nuts' neurotic satisfaction, she would make Hippolyta earn and pay for her death.

Going in on legs which felt as if their bones had turned to melting butter, Alice slammed a hook into Hippolyta's exposed belly. Snatching the gloves from her gory face, the woman blundered backwards and folded over. Although doing so called for a tremendous effort of will, Alice darted after her opponent. Bounding from the mat, the deputy whipped up her left leg. Just in time she remembered that her feet were bare. So she pointed her toes downwards and the top of her instep caught Hippolyta's forehead.

Lifted erect, the woman pitched to the rear at a run and collided with the wall. Alice landed and stumbled, dropping to her right knee and supporting her weight with her hands pressed upon the mat. Hippolyta slumped helplessly against the wall, knees bent and hands trailing limply by her sides.

'Get up!' Burgenhof ordered, almost squeaking in his excitement. 'Finish her off!'

With his emotions racing at full tilt, the man had practically forgotten that Hippolyta was his wife. All through the fight, he had alternated between making sure that the camera was pointing in the correct direction to capture every piece of the action and looking past it to feast his eyes on the scene. His whole body was quivering with the surge of the psychotic agitation caused by what he was seeing. It was the kind of situation he had long dreamed about and he wanted to witness the ultimate satisfaction of a decisive victory; by whom he did not care, just as long as one of the women fighting for his favours went down in complete defeat.

Although the reaction had not been caused by Burgenhof's prompting, Alice regained her feet. Her every instinct warned that she could not continue for much longer. If she hoped to finish off the woman, she must do it while strength and will remained operative. Gritting her teeth, the redhead moved grimly towards the apparently defenceless woman.

Keening softly in torment, Hippolyta had not moved. Yet the brief respite had given her the opportunity to regain a little of her strength. Throbbing in every inch of her body with bitter agony, she had heard and understood what her husband had said. Knowing the words had not been directed at her, they gave the stimulus she needed to make one final, desperate bid for victory.

Just a moment too late, Alice noticed that Hippolya's sagging knees were straightening. Then the woman's right leg rose into the air. Like Alice, Hippolyta knew the danger of kicking with the bare foot. So she had bent her ankle and the ball of her foot thudded under the red head's left breast. Instantly the whole basement seemed to burst into a cauldron of boiling, white hot fire around Alice. Not even able to scream, she stumbled away from Hippolyta. Through the mists that tears of pain and dizziness swirled before her eyes, Alice saw the woman thrust away from the wall and move towards her.

*   *   *

An examination of the door told Brad that it would not be the formidable obstacle he had feared. In fact, he felt certain that he could open it quickly if not quietly.

Flexing his left leg and taking his weight on its foot, Brad prepared to make his entrance. Raising his right leg to the height of the other knee, he pivoted to the left. Bringing into play all the massive power of his gluteus muscles, he threw all his weight behind his right foot as it hurled towards the door. Struck just beneath it with considerable force, the Yale lock sprang open and allowed the door to swing inwards. With only the brief pause required to regain his equilibrium, Brad leaped into the basement.

Although he had expected something of the sort, the big blond skidded to a halt and stared in horror at the two women on the mat. Alice had just taken the kick to the bust and Hippolyta was stumbling dazedly towards her. Both of them looked as badly marked as Hippolyta had in the 'double knock-out' photographs; except that this time the injuries had not been faked with stage make-up.

The momentary hesitation almost cost Brad his life.

Letting out a furious snarl at the intrusion, Burgenhof sprang away from the camera. He landed in the F.B.I. combat crouch which had served him so well on three occasions. The Smith and Wesson moved as if drawn by the attraction of a magnet on the centre of the blond giant's massive chest.

Only one thing saved Brad from sharing Jake Melnick's fate. Sexually stimulated by the fight he had witnessed, Burgenhof was almost on the verge of orgasm. It came, with a sudden force that caused his whole body to jerk, just as he was squeezing the revolver's trigger. The two inch barrel turned just far enough to make the lead which spun from its rifling grooves almost miss its mark.

Brad felt as if something hot had dealt him a glancing kick on the side. A sharp pain bit at him, but it was nowhere near enough to seriously discommode him. Even without orders from his brain, the trained gun-fighter's reflexes had set his body in motion. With his feet slightly apart and knees crooked a little, he tilted his torso to the rear as if speed-rocking the automatic from his forward-raked Bianchi Cooper-Combat bikini belt holster. Locking his right elbow tight against his ribs, with his forearm parallel to the floor, he pointed and started to fire the Colt.

Inflamed by rage at what had happened to Alice, the blond giant acted without any other thought than repaying the hurts she had suffered. So he squeezed the trigger again and again, until eight empty cases* had come hurtling through the ejection slot and the slide stayed in the rearwards position to warn him that the magazine was empty.

The tempest of flying lead, in the form of hand-loaded, ultra-powerful cartridges propelling bullets shaped like truncated cones, blasted Burgenhof's slender body across the basement. Torn almost to doll-rags, and probably dead when the second bullet struck home, the small man crashed in a heap by the wall.

Slowly Brad's head cleared and his eyes dropped to the empty pistol. Then he swung around to help his partner.

As Hippolyta came into range, moving on dragging feet and without raising her hands, Alice lashed out with all her remaining power. The left glove banged sullenly against the woman's battered face. Once more Hippolyta retreated until her back made contact with the wall. Wavering almost mindlessly, with the floor seeming to pitch and heave under her feet, Alice went across the mat. She was no longer conscious of her actions, but her fists continued to flail. At first they beat at Hippolyta's unfeeling head and body. When the woman's feet slid forward and she slipped into a sitting position, propped up by the wall, Alice's gloves continued to strike at where she had been.

From a long way off, or so it seemed, Alice heard a voice telling her to stop. She wondered, not caring greatly in her pain, how soon it would be before Burgenhof enforced the demand by putting a bullet into her back. Then everything went black and Alice did not feel the landing as she collapsed on top of the unconscious Hippolyta.

Although its operator lay dead, the camera's mechanism continued to turn and it was aimed at the two women. Burgenhof would never know, but he had recorded what was practically the double knock-out sequence that he and Hippolyta had planned. Except for one detail, that is. The ending of the fight had not needed to be faked.

Brad had dropped the flashlight when struck by Burgenhof's bullet. He used his empty left hand to explore the extent of his injuries. Looking down, he found that he had a

* Brad's standard loading was seven in the magazine and one in the chamber.

bloody furrow across his side. His torso throbbed as it had the day he had been thrown by a bucking horse and broke a rib.

'Jack's going to love Alice and me,' Brad mused, guessing that he was suffering from a similar injury. 'Both of us on sick leave and him short handed.'

With that, he freed the automatic's cocking slide. Returning the gun to its holster, he went to give his partner first aid. Voices shouted from the ground floor and feet thudded on the basement's stairs. Brad let out a sigh of relief. Help had arrived and Alice would soon be receiving qualified medical attention.

CHAPTER SEVENTEEN

SUPPORTED by a stack of pillows, Joan Hilton looked at Alice Fayde, Brad Counter and Sam Cuchilo as they gathered around her bed in a room at the Central Receiving Hospital. It was a week after the conclusion of the 'Mark' and Hippolyta case, and the blonde was sufficiently recovered to welcome a visit from her friends.

They were friends, not just business acquaintances making a courtesy call. That showed in the pleasure on their faces, even more than in the massive basket of fruit and two enormous bunches of flowers carried by her visitors.

After the inevitable greetings, mingled with demands that she quit faking and came back to help with the routine work of the case, Joan asked to be told everything that had happened after she had been attacked.

'You look like you had fun bringing them in,' Joan commented, looking at Alice. The marks of the fight had not yet left the redhead's face. 'Or has Brad been giving you a licking?'

'No, ma'am,' the big blond declared. 'And, after what I saw her do to that Hippolyta gal, I'm not about to try it.'

Disposing of their gifts, the trio pulled up chairs. Then Alice told Joan all the details which had not been given out to the news media.

'The Houston Police Department sent "Mark's" name along with a couple of others who'd moved down to Gusher City,' the redhead went on, after covering their own activities. 'It arrived on Tuesday—'

'Better late than never,' Joan grinned, thinking of the times when the G.C.P.D. or the Sheriff's Office had been requested for information and sent it too late to be of assistance.

'We passed them a couple of bullets fired through Burgenhof's Luger,' Alice continued. 'So now they can write off their mugger killings.'

'And the theft of those licence plates,' Brad reminded his partner. 'Burgenhof knew about the consignment and stole them to keep switching plates on his Jeepster. Nobody at the Houston Steel Products' head office suspected him.'

'How did you find out about that?' Joan inquired.

'Hippolyta told us,' Alice replied. 'She offered a full confession if we'd let her write up the stories of the fights she'd had for *Pussy-Grapple* magazine. It was worth it to tie up all the loose ends. Anyways, writing keeps her quiet in the cells.'

'Even without her confession, we could make her for the Zekov kill,' Cuchilo commented. 'Give Burgenhof his due, he was a damned good cameraman. We developed all his movies and have the whole bit, how Hippolyta threw Della with a monkey climb and she bust her neck when she landed.'

'What's happened to the movies?' Joan wanted to know.

'They're being held for evidence,' Alice explained.

'Including the one with you and her?'

'That too. The sheriff thinks we should have it in case the defence attorney starts trying to enlist public sympathy by claiming we worked her over out of revenge.'

'Now *that's* one movie I aim to see,' Joan promised. 'And when I get the chance, I'm going to shake Hippolyta's hand.'

'What for?' Alice asked, oozing innocence despite guessing what was coming.

'For saving me from having to beat you up,' Joan answered. "I heard what's happened to my car.'

'Don't worry, white sister,' Cuchilo grunted, in his most impressive 'noble Hollywood redman' manner. 'Me got friend, heap big medicine man. Him light spirit fire, sing powerful medicine song. And, seeing that he owns the best garage in Rockabye County, he'll make that beat-up old ruin almost as good as new.'

'They do say it's hard to get spares for a *1801* Model T like that,' Alice remarked.

'Happen it's not made even better than when I left it,' Joan warned, 'I'm going to trade it in for a Ford Mustang, Miss Fayde. Yours.' Having delivered the threat, she glared at Brad. 'Why did you have to get into that basement so quick? I bet Hippolyta was whipping her good.'

'It was a close thing, ma,' Alice announced, sounding like a punch-drunk boxer addressing a newscaster's microphone. 'But we sure won.'

'Hey though!' Cuchilo ejaculated. 'Do you know whose house the Burgenhofs were living in?'

'One of your blasted war lodge's chief's I'd not be surprised,' Joan replied. 'All right, I'm too sick, feeble and tired to play guessing games.'

'It was one that Hermie Sheen had fitted out for his floating crap games,' the Comanche replied. 'He was figuring to use it for his biggest game and had had it built with that in mind.'

'Why didn't somebody think of it.' Joan demanded.

'It's one that we didn't find out about,' Cuchilo told her. 'He was killed by the Syndicate before he could get it open.'

'Burgenhof couldn't have found a better place for his caper if he'd tried every street in the city,' Alice declared. 'It had been built by out-of-town help. Not even the real estate agents who handled it had any idea what it was to be used for. He says that he was only too pleased to get it off his hands, the Widow Sheen was asking a higher price than most folks would pay for that neck of the woods.'

'You know something?' Alice remarked. 'If he hadn't been such a bad *hombre*. I could almost have felt sorry for Burgenhof.'

'Most times when we talk about a bad *hombre*, we mean a big, powerful, vicious and ruthless crook with a temper like a stick-teased diamondback rattler's,' Joan commented. 'But Burgenhof was only a little feller.'

'Little or not,' Alice replied. 'He was one bad *hombre*.'

Read more about the team of Alice Fayde and Bradford Counter in
THEY CALL IT PROGRESS
the next Rockabye County story.